SEPTEMBER THOMAS

War of Earth

The Elemental Gods Book Four

First edition

ISBN: 978-1-7342545-3-2

Editing by Fiona McLaren
Cover art by Natasha MacKenzie

This book was professionally typeset on Reedsy.
Find out more at reedsy.com

For Sydney

Chapter 1

I drew my jacket tight around my shoulders, less to combat the chill brought by the light spring breeze and more as a shield against the tension radiating from the incubus at my side. Still, I shivered as the haze of rank sweat on my skin cooled, the sensation doing nothing to soothe the burn that ached deep within me.

"Another nightmare?" Ryder asked.

Laughter drifted up from the street four stories below. I glanced down from where I perched on the roof. A woman a little older than me with a yellow bob and a scarlet dress splashed through the rainwater pooling in the gutter from the passing storm. She called out in German to a guy meandering behind her, her strappy high heels dangling from his hand at his side.

It felt surreal, the normalcy of the courtship playing out before us, when just ten minutes ago I'd woken alone on a creaky twin bed in a shoebox of a room, hands smashed against my lips, nails digging pinprick grooves into my skin, choking back screams.

"When *don't* I have nightmares, is the better question," I replied. My attempt at levity fell flat.

The woman who ran this fey hostel had warned Lachlan and me against coming up to the roof when we'd arrived in Munich two days ago. As an incubus, Ryder could sprout wings or scatter his molecules into millions of particles of dust, so he was safe if he tumbled from the open sides. With his tipped ears and willowy stance, most realized Lach was an elf; she knew he didn't have any powers that could save him from a fall unless someone was foolish enough to hand over some of their magic. What she hadn't guessed was how frequently I happened to be that fool.

With my face concealed in the shadows of my hood and my magical signature intentionally muddled, she hadn't identified me as one of the four teenage Gods tasked with saving the world from destruction. She hadn't known I was the only one of those four Gods with control over three elements at my fingertips.

One of those handy elements being Air.

"Do you want to talk about it?" Ryder's voice drew me back. I blinked up at his profile, at the shadow of stubble darkening his jaw, at his thin lips set in a straight, firm line. I tried to remember the last time those lips had curved in a smile and couldn't.

"What?" I asked dumbly.

"About your nightmare." His brows pinched with worry. Silvery beams of moonlight cast long shadows in the hollows beneath his eyes and danced like white fire in the highlights of his hair, transforming him from the man I knew into the wicked fey prince he was supposed to be—a façade he'd cast aside long ago. "Do you want to talk about it?"

Ryder always asked me if I wanted to talk whenever I woke up—whether I shocked myself awake or if he shook me from the nightmares himself. I threaded my fingers through my hair, wincing at the slick greasiness of the strands.

He knew I almost always dreamed of eyes.

And voices. Angry, accusatory voices of loved ones I'd lost, berating me for what I had and hadn't done, slicing me open in a way bullets and blades never could.

But last night had been different. Worse, somehow, in its unexpectedness.

"I dreamed I was Ridley," I admitted.

Ryder's jaw clenched, the tendons in his neck tightening like thick cables. This time, when he reached for my hand, I didn't pull away. "Tell me."

Incapable of maintaining the intensity in his gaze, I looked down. The dusty red brick rimming the rooftop crumbled in spots and entire sections were missing in others—victims of age and time.

I struggled to describe the perspective of what I'd witnessed in my sleep.

"It... we... I was back in the cabin where the witches had sealed the curse." A curse that, until three weeks ago, had threatened to strip first daemoni like Ryder of their magic, and then consume magic altogether. "The witches were dead, but I wasn't me. I was Ridley. The knife that cut my soul from my body—" My shoulders hunched, recalling the acidic burn in my blood, the sizzling agony that surged in vindictive intensity. "I felt it destroying me from the inside out."

A car horn blared, reminding me I wasn't, in fact, still strapped in that awful place. The callouses on Ryder's thumb grounded me as it traced circles on the back of my hand.

"I could hear me—the real me, not the Ridley-me—arguing with Kaleal about what to do, but I don't remember what I said in response." While I recalled the desperation in my voice, I couldn't remember the words, as if cotton plugged my ears.

"The next thing I knew, the room went up in flames. Fire spread everywhere." My fingers twitched. I thought of the ripple of the scarlet sea engulfing the floor, the roar of hungry flames devouring the ceiling, the crackle of beams as they crumbled to ash. Flames *I* had created to destroy the curse created by the witches so their work would never be replicated.

Flames I had abandoned to devour the soul of a prince I'd never had time to understand.

"I couldn't stop it and I couldn't move. Between the lightning splitting my soul and the burning of my skin… there wasn't anything I could do." My breath rattled against my ribs. "I was dying… and I'd accepted that."

Ryder finally caved to his instincts and drew me against him, hand curling around my side as he pressed me close. His cheek rested on top of my head, and I relented, accepting his quiet comfort, my palm flat against the muscles of his chest. I allowed myself a minute to soak in his smoke and cinnamon scent, steeling myself for what came next.

"I remember looking up, right before the end," I said. "I saw someone standing there, standing over me. A shadowy figure untouched by the destruction. I saw their eyes." My fingers curled into claws, threatening to tear Ryder's Henley, wishing I could crawl inside him to escape the ugliness inside me.

"My eyes."

Not Kaleal's violet eyes, like I'd anticipated—for she, too, haunted my dreams. *My* eyes.

I peered up through the heavy sweep of my lashes, imagining the aquamarine shimmer of my eerie gaze, remembering their hard edge that had cut through me—like twine through gelatin—in the dream.

"I said something…" I pressed two fingers to my chapped lips, trying to recreate the words they'd shaped in the moments before consciousness claimed me. "Then I woke up."

Beneath my palm, Ryder's heart hammered.

This wasn't the first time I'd dreamed of Ridley. The former Prince of Sin often worked his way into my thoughts. Sometimes we discussed trivial topics, my brain searching for hidden meanings. Other times, darker times that made heat curl sensually in my chest, I explored the depths of the single kiss we'd shared. A kiss as sultry as it was confusing.

Ridley also frequently joined the voices in my head, shouting my

4

insecurities for what felt like the world to hear.

This, though, marked the first time I'd inhabited Ridley's body. The first time I'd not only watched his final moments but *lived* them.

"I wish I could take these memories from you," Ryder finally said.

I stared at the crisscross stitching of his shirt and swiped at my nose with the back of my hand, incapable of looking at him in the rawness of the aftermath of the memory.

"I wish the battle with the witches had gone differently, that somehow both you and my brother could have made it out alive. And when the decision to… leave him was made…" A thread of agony strangled his voice. He cleared his throat. "I wish I could have somehow taken your place. But I couldn't and I can't."

He tapped the underside of my chin, quietly asking me to look at him. I considered resisting, then relented, drawn in by the earnestness etched in every line of his body. "But I'm here now. And I'm glad you told me about this."

I smoothed his black shirt where my nails had dug grooves in the fabric, then released him, needing to put some space between us. Beside me, the air conditioning unit clicked on, humming softly.

He said the words, but I wasn't sure how much he meant them. As confident as he was in himself, and as indifferent as he tried to seem about Ridley's passing, I knew Ryder was deeply rattled by what had happened, though he never seemed to want to talk about it.

Or about the frequency of Ridley's appearances in my dreams.

Ryder moved to the corner of the roof, fingers shoveling through his hair, and released his other, darker side. His skin blackened to bullet-proof granite and leathery, bat-like wings spread wide behind him. I imagined he appeared more abandoned gargoyle than forgotten prince in that moment.

I rolled the sleeve of my battered olive jacket to my elbow, methodically tapping the many black bands that looked like tattooed bracelets on my skin. They were actually oaths: magical pledges fey made to one another when debts were owed. As I tapped each unique band, I recalled the fey who'd sworn it and the circumstances behind it.

With each tap, the tension knotting my shoulders relaxed a fraction.

I inhaled, relishing the clean quality of the air, the pollution of the city washed away with the passing of the recent storm, and felt a little stronger for it.

"What do you think this means?" I asked, broaching the one topic we'd deliberately avoided, hoping it would eventually fade. Instead, it lingered like the stink of skunk. "The dreams?"

Ryder sank to a crouch as I walked up beside him, the gravel on the roof crunching beneath my scarred black boots. The edge of one silky wing brushed my arm, sending goosebumps darting across my skin. "That question is complicated."

"Uncomplicate it for me." I tugged the vial hanging from a fine chain around my neck out from beneath the collar of my shirt and spun it, pads of my fingers finding the familiar shapes of the silver encasing the glass. "Since whatever this is, is happening to me, I deserve to know."

He exhaled loudly through his nose. "The short answer: I don't know what the dreams mean. The long answer: I've never heard of any krav legara partners who never mutually completed the bond."

The idea of krav legara was still new to me. It was unique to daemoni, who relied on lust and sin to fuel their powers and to survive. Typically, daemoni could only form relationships with those of their own kind, or else they risked draining them dry. Krav legara were unique fey outside of the daemoni who could stand up to their abilities, who didn't die when their partners sampled their souls.

I'd been told the odds of finding a partner like that were thin.

I'd been told the daemoni considered it a sacred bond, second to none.

Then again, the prince who'd told me that also accepted his half of that very bond he shared with me for his own selfish purposes... and had died soon after.

While I understood he'd accepted the bond as the only way he could think of to save his people, I wished I'd had the time to ask him to explain his rationale. I wanted to know if he'd considered the ramifications of his decision.

If he'd thought about what it might mean for me.

But it was far too late to ask him now.

I kicked at some of the crumbling brick, listening to it rattle as it dropped to the pavement below. It might be too late to ask Ridley his thoughts, but that didn't mean it was too late to figure out things with Ryder. And I desperately needed to hear from him now.

"Please talk to me," I begged. "Please help me understand. What happens to partners who do mutually complete the bond and one of them dies?"

Ryder relented and scrubbed his forehead. "The survivor typically doesn't last very long. They've lost half their soul. Granted, not many take their own life outright, but they self-destruct in other ways like making riskier decisions or withering away silently."

"But I didn't accept the bond," I argued. "What happens then?"

"I don't know."

"And then there's—" I bit my tongue, barged ahead anyway. "And then there's you. I was bound to you, too." Was being the operative word. Since the battle with the witches, neither Ryder nor I had felt the magical hum of the connection that had strung us together like wire between two electrical poles. We weren't sure if it was gone or now lay dormant, but we couldn't access it, regardless. "Shouldn't that mean something? Wouldn't that help me, somehow?"

Ryder dug his teeth into his lower lip, closed his eyes as if in pain. "I don't know."

A greasy, oily sensation pooled in my stomach. "I didn't want this,

Ryder. I didn't want to be caught in the middle of this mess. There are so many bigger things than this—stopping the apocalypse. Kaleal. Finding Marinda. And yet, I can't stop wondering about what this means."

Thunder burbled overhead. I cursed and flicked my hand, dismissing the billowing black clouds. I hadn't meant to lure the storm back to the city.

I dropped to the edge of the roof beside Ryder so hard it bruised my hip and drew my legs up tight to my chest. The forty-foot drop didn't bother me like it would have when I'd been just another human. Ryder's wings spread wide, engulfing me in heat.

"Sometimes I wonder if Ridley is living inside me," I admitted. "Like I brought part of him back when I summoned the Thunderbird to escape his decaying mind. Do you… do you think that could be possible?"

"I don't know, Zara."

I closed my eyes against the frostiness of Ryder's tone.

"I don't know what any of this means. I don't know what is or isn't possible. And I don't know how to fix it or if it can be fixed," he raged, my frustration sparking his. "What I do know is that whatever connected us before has snapped.

"And now you confuse the sin out of me. Sometimes we're like this." He motioned at the six inches of space between our bodies. "Like nothing has changed. And sometimes you're as distant as Mars and just as mysterious."

It hurt, the words spitting from his lips like sparks from a bonfire. But each syllable rang with truth. I *had* pulled away from him since the fight. As irrational as it was, I had felt some tingling sense of betrayal when I fell into the easiness that was being around him.

I'd backed away in an attempt to understand what that meant on my own terms, to not complicate Ryder's life more than I already had.

I hadn't considered I might be hurting matters more than I was helping them.

"I miss being able to sense your emotions because, Zara, stars, you hide them from yourself as much as you hide them from everyone else." The incubus balled his fists on his thighs. "And I want to help you deal with everything that's happened because…"

He cracked his knuckles, each pop crisp as a cap pried from a bottle. "Because part of me thinks that if I can help you heal, that I'll heal myself."

Chapter 2

A vicious, gaping wound slashed open inside me, one that fountained pain like scalding water from a geyser. I ignored the part of me clamoring to keep my distance, and closed the gap between us, plastering myself against Ryder's side. His body heaved once, evidence of the war raging inside him, before he wrapped his emotions up tight.

Like he accused me of doing.

I knew it was wrong to ask this of him when there were parts of me I still wasn't willing to lay out in the open, but it was also wrong to allow him to suffer through this alone. Not when I still hoped to resolve things between us. "Will you tell me what's going through your head right now?"

His jaw worked, and he stared somewhere over my head. "I didn't think he could die." Silence swelled. "As a kid, I always saw Ridley as this invincible, immovable force. He was so proud and so commanding and he was never, ever—" Ryder's teeth gnashed—"wrong. He raised me and then when he turned his back on me, without so much as asking what I was going through…"

His fingers flexed, and I reached for him, squeezing the icy digits hard in my fist.

Ryder continued, "I hated what Ridley did to me, what he said to me, but that didn't mean he wasn't still my brother."

I hesitated, then dug deep down, stirring the golden embers I'd avoided since burning down the cabin, stoking them, passing their comforting warmth from my hand to his. The incubus jolted, the skin around his eyes tightening, but he didn't let go. Wouldn't let go.

"I always thought I'd have more time. That one day he would reach out to me, or that I'd stumble across him, and we'd figure out our mess." The wind picked up and the door to the stairwell we'd propped open with a brick creaked. "Turns out we didn't. We didn't fix things. And then he had the gall to betray me *again*. And now—with you—and how twisted things are…"

Ryder released me and stood, boots thudding as he stepped back. He shoved his hands through his hair over and over again, refusing to finish his sentence.

I gave him his moment, wishing I had the words to solve this, yet nothing of great significance came to mind. Sticky mud still clung to my insides, holding me hostage, no matter how hard I tried to pull free. I knew how I had felt about him, and I knew how I felt now—and didn't know what to think.

In the back of my mind, a smokey presence swirled, an anaconda unwinding from a nap, ready to take on another day and devour the prey that came with it.

Kaleal.

The Original God of Water.

An ancient soul who so inconveniently shared my body.

The heels of my boots rapped against the side of the building, knocking tiny chunks of brick free. A series of dents alongside mine indicated others had done this same thing over the years and decades. This hostel was one strong windstorm away from toppling.

It hadn't taken Kaleal long to crack the rune binding her to a room inside my head this time. I'd voluntarily broken that seal once already, and while my witchy friend Lee had tried to repair it, neither of us had expected it to hold.

However, since freeing herself the day we left Vegas, she'd been strangely subdued. The cynical, haughty voice that had underscored my thoughts for months only echoed inside my head once or twice a day. I knew better than to relax under the lack of scrutiny. My walls remained high, my hackles raised.

She must be up to something.

I wasn't naïve enough to think Kaleal would sit back and relax, though I wished she would have stayed asleep for a few more minutes.

"Ryder?"

The incubus turned, hands still shoved deep in his hair. His cheeks had hollowed and lines I didn't recognize fanned from his eyes. He had hundreds of years of experience on me, yet he'd never seemed particularly aged until this moment. This moment where he wrestled with his past... and his present. "Yes?"

More brick crumbled as I drew my legs back up to the ledge and stood, needing to be on my feet. He hadn't asked me yet, and it probably wasn't fair of me to ask, but the question soared around us on hawk's wings.

"Have your feelings about me changed?" I jammed my hands into my jacket pockets, hoping to hide how tightly I clenched my fingers. I couldn't meet his gaze, couldn't bear to watch the dance of emotions—or lack thereof—across his face.

"Sin, Zara, I—" His head dropped back, chest rising and falling rapidly. The black haze that was his magic blurred the edges of his form.

One minute stretched into two. Four.

I fought to keep my breathing even, despite the wild kicking of my heart. It hurt. The waiting. I hadn't expected this question to hurt so much. Ryder had always been so firm in his beliefs, so in-tune with his emotions—especially where they pertained to me—that this sudden hesitation caught me off-guard.

12

Overhead, billions of stars winked and blinked against their backdrop of blue-black, seemingly growing larger by the second, closing in on us. Caging us in.

Finally, I couldn't take it anymore. The words burst from my mouth like a dam bursting under a 100-year flood. "Never mind. That wasn't fair of me. I shouldn't have asked that. I'm sorry. I—"

Ryder's hand landed heavily on my shoulder, freezing my thought. His thumb traced the jut of my collarbone, drifted up the side of my neck, nudging my chin up again. I bit down on my fears, wrapping them together in a tight lasso, and looked up. Amber eyes reflected my inner turmoil, revealing a blend of anxiety, agony, and—tenderness.

"Don't apologize. Never apologize for asking me things, for telling me what's on your mind. I need to know what you're thinking." He smoothed my hair behind my ears, his eyes following the motions. "I want to tell you I care for you as I've always cared for you, ever since I knew what you meant to me from the night we met, but that would be a lie."

I sucked in a rattling gasp, a well-aimed knife slicing between my ribs, puncturing the tender organs beneath. Gusts of wind picked up, tugging at our clothing, and a thin layer of ice formed at my feet. I'd expected something like this, but I hadn't prepared myself to hear the words out loud.

Ryder shook me, drawing me back to the moment. "Don't drift away yet. I'm not done."

Oh stars. It got worse.

Mentally I berated myself, ordering myself to not run off, to not fly away, to not wrap myself in a cocoon of water and hide for the next thousand years. Kaleal shifted forward, silent on her ghostly legs, eager to hear the words that would grind my fragile heart into a paste.

"The bond broke," I murmured through numb lips. "I understand."

His expression softened, and he risked a step forward on the slick concrete, leaving a spare few inches between our bodies. "No, you don't, glowstick. I don't care about you as I did all those months ago, because those emotions pale in comparison to how I feel now."

The nerves skating across my arms stilled. The wind stilled. The concrete dried. My numbness vanished, and I felt hyperaware of everything that touched my skin, every whorl of his fingerprints, every warm puff of his breath.

He what?

"I knew *what* you were to me, but not *who* you were," he whispered. "Over the past year, I've seen you face incredibly difficult odds and overcome them at every count—rising above every challenge with the grace I've come to associate as inherently *you*. I admire your loyalty, your tenacity, your unbreakable spirit."

His fingers carded through the hair at the back of my head. "I've held you while you broke and backed you when you took a stand. I've watched you grow, finding yourself in a mess of a world that won't stop throwing punches. I've watched you fight like fury for what you believe in, and I've watched love fill you to bursting. I've seen that love drive you to protect others, even when it would be easier if you didn't."

My limbs tingled with warmth, a warmth so unlike the flames that flickered in my belly, a warmth I hadn't known I could ever feel—I ever *needed* to feel. My world became the golden glow of his eyes, the honey of his voice. A centaur could have clattered up the side of the building and riddled us full of arrows, and I wouldn't have noticed.

"Yes, the bond is broken." A muscle jumped in his jaw. "But that's ok, because what I know about you, what I *feel* for you… has grown so much bigger than all that. How I feel, Zara, it's so much larger than fate."

I closed the gap between us, rising on my toes. His chest shuddered against mine as I hooked the back of his neck, bringing our faces impossibly close. I'd never wanted a kiss so badly, and the shaking of his arms around me showed me how much he agreed. I leaned forward, but he pulled back, squeezing his eyes closed with a pained groan.

"But there are other consequences of the bond breaking," he said. The joy humming through my veins diminished. "Physical consequences."

I lowered, flat-footed again. "What are you saying?"

"The bond allowed us to be physical without the risk of you losing parts of your soul." Ryder gripped the zippered edges of my jacket that draped open. "With that gone, I'm not sure I can restrain myself, especially given the draw of your magic.

"I meant what I said in Kansas City. I believe I can draw enormous amounts of power from you without consequence because of what you are. You are one of four beings channeling the magic that forms the core of the world. But your soul..." He tapped the center of my chest, expression fracturing. "I'm not willing to risk."

I felt torn in two, half of me elated at the words that had spilled so beautifully from his lips mere moments ago and half of me shocked, grieving, pained by the reality he painted. He wanted me. But he couldn't have me.

And I...

Ryder sighed. "And you have not yet made your decision about what I mean to you."

Frost glazed over my insides, quelling the flames he'd fanned into life. "You're wrong."

His brow lifted.

"I like you, well... more than like you. I know I feel lighter when you're around, and my heart flutters when we touch. I know I can't wait to see you when I wake up—and I don't think that ever had anything to do with the bond. Even with Ridley complicating things there..." My thoughts gained speed, tripping over each other as I struggled to figure out what I was trying to say.

"I never loved Ridley. I never got to know him for long enough to find out if I could feel anything for him." My hand curled at my chest. "But I respected him. I value the lessons he taught me, but I won't ever be able to forgive him for what he did to me back at the Bellagio, when he sicced Rim on me like a dog, invading my head." I gripped the sides of my skull, remembering the way I'd shattered that day, splintered open from the inside out.

"I trusted Ridley when he said he only wanted the best for his people." I swallowed. "But what was best for his people did not mean what was best for me. And Ryder… you've done nothing but put what's best for me first."

Hope bloomed bright on Ryder's face. My chest swelled, hot and sticky with emotion, but I carefully took a step back. "But I'm not ready to commit yet. There's so much more to do. We can't rush this."

Ryder's hands fisted in his pockets, and he swung his head to stare down at the street below.

You're so weak, Kaleal murmured in my thoughts. *I'll never know what you see in him, in any of the daemoni, really, but if you can't figure out your emotions after that confession—*

Shut up, I ordered. *I never asked your opinion.*

Always so touchy.

"I think we both need to reconcile a few things within ourselves first," I explained. "I need to find Marinda and figure out what she means to me. And you need to settle decades of resentment… and then there's the whole—" my throat clicked and heat washed across my cheeks— "physical thing you mentioned. I think we'll get there, but I also think there's no point in rushing anything right now."

"That's fair." Ryder had closed in again, drawn to me like magnetic pieces. "We'll figure out some of those details, and while we sort all that out… I promised you before, I wasn't going anywhere. I fully intend to stand by that."

The corners of my lips turned up. I opened my mouth to respond when another voice came from the open door to the stairwell.

"Seriously, how do I always end up in the middle of your mushy moments?"

Chapter 3

Ryder's eyes rolled upward, sending a silent plea toward some unknown entity. I pressed the heel of my hand to my forehead and turned to the door.

"We weren't doing anything, Lachlan," I sighed. "There's literally two feet of space between us." Maybe it was closer to three feet, but who was counting? Ryder hopped from the ledge, advancing on the elf, who lounged against the doorframe, spooning yogurt into his mouth.

"That's the fourth time you've interrupted us," Ryder said. I huffed and dropped behind him. There went my argument. "And I sensed you watching for a full minute before saying anything. If I didn't know any better, I'd say you've got a thing for—"

"The pheromones must be messing with your brain, Ry." Lach spooned another glob of yellow goo into his mouth before pointing at the incubus with the utensil. "No universe exists where I would ever want to be caught in the middle of you making out—"

"—not making out," I butted in, still processing Ryder's allegation.

"—or doing *more* than making out," Lachlan continued, waggling the spoon suggestively. I threw my hands in the air. "Or discussing personal relations or *anything* along those lines. As far as I'm concerned, the more distance between the two of you, the better off we all are."

He turned the spoon on Ryder. "You know, I'm not entirely sure if you're needed here. Sure you aren't needed somewhere distant? Like

18

Hong Kong? Then the boss and I—"

The incubus snatched the spoon from Lach's hand and flung it over the side of the roof. The elf blinked, pale brows twitching, shrugged, and drew another spoon from his sleeve. Probably alongside the needlelike daggers he kept handy. "You're so petty. One little comment and you turn all beast mode."

"Would you shut up already?" I zapped Lach with a tiny bolt of lightning that was little more than static. "No one asked you to come up here."

Ryder pointed at me with his thumb. "What she said."

The edge of Lach's spoon grated against the sides of his plastic cup, but he kept his mouth shut. Belatedly, I realized he'd probably wanted me to use magic on him so he could steal some of it.

My eyes narrowed.

The elf grinned cockily.

Sneaky bastard.

"Where were you, anyway?" I asked the elf. A thought occurred to me, a tingle of curiosity I'd forgotten about in the wake of the nightmare. "Hold up. Where were *both* of you?" Ryder's smirk faded, his expression falling flat. "Lach, I'm used to you taking off in the middle of the night, but Ryder, what were you doing?"

"Ha." Lach adjusted his baseball cap, strawberry blond hair curling around the edges, and pointed at the incubus. "What she said."

Ryder shot a ripple of darkness at the elf, who dispersed the particles with a swipe of his hand. Lach tsked. "Remember that beast mode comment I made earlier?"

Ryder responded with a snarl, skin blackening as talons burst from his fingers, and he launched himself at Lachlan, who brought up his fisted arms in self-defense, hopping back and forth like a boxer in the ring. "Let's go!"

"You're going to—"

19

"Boys." A wall of frosted ice exploded into existence between the two. Ryder pulled his punch before his knuckles connected, still glaring at the elf, who jumped and clapped merrily from the safety of his alcove. The start of a headache pounded in my temples. "Would you *pretend* like you like each other for half a second and *focus?*"

They'd been like this since we'd entered the airport in Las Vegas and Lachlan had swiped Ryder's bag with a wink and an insult, resulting in a scrambling chase through the crowded hallways. It only ended when Lachlan nearly knocked over a sweet-faced woman old enough to be my grandmother's grandmother—who delivered the tongue-lashing of the decade.

Ryder grumbled and brushed invisible dust from his slacks. Lach flicked me a two-fingered salute. "Whatever you say, boss."

I pointed at the incubus, who leveled a steely look at me. "Where were you?"

His foot tapped on the ground, a tic I'd never seen from him before. "I needed a minute to myself. No harm in that."

Lach's brows shot up his forehead. Evasion? That was new. I crossed my arms. "Even Lachlan comes up with better excuses than that."

"Why does it matter so much?" the incubus snapped, then seemed to catch himself. His hand shot behind his neck and the muscles in his arms flexed. "If you have to know, I needed to recharge, ok?"

My stomach swooped, and Lachlan's quirky smile vanished. I'd never thought about that, about how the incubus needed to feed on lust to maintain his strength. Ryder so rarely lost control, so very rarely discussed it, that it never occurred to me it might be a problem.

But if he'd gone out to recharge, what did that mean? Had he… ? I brought that train of thought to a screeching halt. He wouldn't jeopardize things between us, not after what he'd said.

Unless…

I held my tongue, silently pleading for Ryder to fill in the gaps in

20

my knowledge, but he refused to meet my eyes, foot still tapping the gravelly ground. "I went to a club, grabbed a drink, and hung out for an hour." His eyes widened, and he seemed to realize what I was getting at. "That's it, though. I came right back. No detours. I wouldn't—haven't—"

"It's ok." I attempted a weak smile. "If you had—it's not like—we aren't—"

I fumbled with an explanation as I tried to shove the flame of my jealousy into a tiny jar and screw a cap on top, extinguishing the ugly emotion altogether. I didn't have a right to feel jealous. Hadn't I said I wasn't willing to commit to him? That meant Ryder was free to do whatever he wanted with whomever he wanted.

But why hadn't it occurred to me before that he might do just that?

See, you're weak, Kaleal chided. *You won't go after what you want, so you risk losing it. Maybe that's what you deserve.*

I missed the months where I and I alone had been privy to my thoughts.

I banded my arms around myself. If Ryder and I had any hope of resolving our deal here, it started with being open. He'd called me out earlier for hiding my emotions. I needed to change that, and what better time than now?

"Ok, it's not ok. It would have hurt. A lot." My brain couldn't figure out where to look, my eyes dancing from Ryder to Lach to the open doorway to my foot grinding a deeper hole in the rock. "But, like we said, we aren't together and I have no right to expect you to limit your..." I scratched my head, searching for the right word, as the corner of Ryder's mouth lifted marginally.

"Frivolities." I finally supplied, then hurried on. "I hadn't considered your need to feed and that you need to worry about yourself... obviously."

What was I saying? Were those sentences?

Dizziness spun in my head, my arms squeezing so tight my ribs groaned. I tried to remember the words that had come out of my mouth.

That could have gone so much better.

Lachlan barked a laugh. "I wish you could see your face right now, boss. You turned so red—"

"Ignore him," Ryder sighed.

I flicked Ryder a look through my lashes. He still wore that puzzling half-smile that seemed part gleeful and part dazed.

He huffed, shaking his head. "You have nothing to be jealous about, glowstick. I didn't do anything. I hadn't thought about doing anything. And I certainly don't want to do anything with anyone else." His lips tugged higher, revealing his dimple. "But it's doing wonders for me knowing you're jealous."

My mouth dropped open.

"We may have to explore this at a later date." He tapped his chin with mock bemusement. "See what it means in terms of you surrendering to your feelings after all."

Lach groaned, bracing against the ice wall, his forehead resting on the backs of his hands. "Seriously? Did you not hear me earlier?" He raised his head. "Couldn't you at least throat-punch him or something, boss? I know you wanted to. At least that would be entertaining."

He squawked when I melted the ice and he tumbled to his knees into the pool of water. Lach shook his hands, splattering droplets of water everywhere. "That was rude."

"Did you think I'd forgotten about you?" I asked. "What information did you glean tonight?"

The elf forgot all about what he was going to say and leaned back on his heels, his face sparking with sudden energy. A hardened shell of air closed in around the three of us as Lachlan closed off this conversation to only the three of us.

22

He drew open a panel of his coat, reached inside, and withdrew a piece of paper. After a beat, Ryder took it.

"I've found her."

Chapter 4

Mouth dry and head light, I watched Ryder unfold the page. There was only one *her* Lachlan could be talking about. Marinda. The witch who'd helped me escape as an infant from the Palace of Oceans as the Order brought the castle tumbling down. The woman I'd tracked for three weeks across three continents, speaking with every fey who had the slightest recollection of that day.

I knew four things from those I spoke with. Marinda had been the second-in-command at the Palace of Oceans, second only to the High Priestess herself. She was the only known fey to have escaped the castle itself. She had stowed away on a cargo ship to get from Norway to the United States while keeping me hidden. And she'd pulled on an ancient system of favors to secret me to a family in the Midwest who would take care of me.

What happened next, no one knew.

Several fey speculated she died not long after escaping, believing the Order had hunted her down. Others believed she lived in hiding. Some heard she'd succumbed to insanity after sacrificing her own infant daughter to trick the Order long enough to enable our escape.

And now, despite the impossibility of our mission, Lachlan presented a map marked with her precise location. I snatched the document from Ryder. "Tell me everything."

The elf removed his hat and scratched his head. "I know a guy who knows a guy who worked with Marinda to finish the 'transaction'—" he used air quotes— "of finding a suitable family to take care of you until things settled down. He apparently lives here in Munich and agreed to meet with me."

Lach stood and swiped uselessly at his drenched pants. "After some finagling, I got him to admit he knows some nymphs who've monitored Marinda for years." He pointed at the map. "There's a small town at the base of the Carpathian Mountains in Romania. Once we get there, we find a cabin nearest the pine trees to the north end of town. That's where she is."

Ryder snorted.

That didn't sound sketchy *at all.*

The information we'd been looking for conveniently dropped in our laps? Not long after we arrived in Munich? I brought the page closer to my face, frowning at the red circle scribbled in ballpoint pen. "What makes you trust this?"

"Oh, you know." Lach edged around me and perched on the ledge, fingering the edges of his long coat. "It sounded slightly more reasonable than some of the other leads we've gotten." He drew a pair of needle-like knives from his sleeves and examined them. Silvery light glanced off their slender surfaces, turning to moonbeams in his hands, rendering the tips impossible to see.

Give me a break. Kaleal rolled her eyes so hard I thought they might screw out of her head. *Speaking of fey I can't believe you choose to spend your time with... this one is two dares away from selling you out. You control three elements. You took down the Order. You can afford better company.*

I counted to three in my head, forcing myself to not engage with her. Kaleal was wrong about the elf, but I recognized his evasion. "Lach." I stressed the syllable, hand braced at my waist. "What aren't you telling me?"

"What did this information cost us?" Ryder threw in. The door to the stairwell creaked again, but I sensed nothing of concern.

Lachlan dug his pinkie into his ear. "What was that? Couldn't quite hear you there. Maybe—"

"You heard me fine." Ryder held dangerously still. I knew that posture, that tone. Lachlan didn't stand a chance. "Assuming this information is accurate, no one in their right mind would have given it up easily, especially since it's known one of the Gods wants it."

"Oh yes, that, right." Lach scrubbed at his eyebrow. "See, I had to trade a favor, but in the grand scheme of things…"

Ryder strode forward, grabbed Lach's collar, and hefted him into the air, teeth bared in a snarl mere millimeters from Lachlan's own. The elf's knives clattered uselessly to the ground. "Whose favor?"

The incubus truly was in a mood tonight, and Lach was a fool if he kept antagonizing him. The elf's crystal eyes flicked over Ryder's shoulder at me, one side of his lips pulling up in apology. "Come on, do you really think he wanted a favor from me?"

Ryder pulled back his fist, holding Lach up with one arm, but I snagged his elbow before he could throw the punch. Frost tinted the tips of my fingers in a warning and he stared at me, muscles fluttering in his jaw, questions burning on his face.

"Drop him." I felt for Phenex's vial, sliding the fine links of the chain back and forth across the back of my neck. "And let him explain."

Silence settled, soft as snow, before the airtight bubble of silence shattered. Ryder dropped Lach, who caught himself before he fell. A driver on the street below laid on the horn, shouting curses at someone who responded, slinging heated slurs. Somewhere else, a door opened, and pounding, bass-heavy music spilled out before it closed again.

Lach tugged on his coat, straightening his collar, and appealed to me. "You told me I could barter with your favors. That's why I trust this guy. He said he would tell me what I needed to know in exchange for one favor sworn in the form of an oath. If his information didn't pan out, the oath would break." He rubbed his jaw, shooting glances at the incubus. "That's the only reason why I thought his information was good."

Ryder had been against trading oaths since the start, arguing the ask was too much for information we could probably get another way. However, I'd argued that to get the information I wanted within any reasonable period of time, I'd likely have to trade something for it. Something big.

Whatever it was about this woman that drew me to her, I knew I didn't want to wait. Hearing her name from the lips of those cursed witches had released something inside me. A drive that wouldn't subside.

"He did what I asked him to do," I said at last. I hooked my hands behind my neck, staring up at the wispy clouds moving in as if they bore the answers I sought. Their twisting tendrils looked a little like the Kraken's tentacles.

Marinda was more than a name, she was a key part of my past. She represented a vital piece of the puzzle that had created me, that had cast me into the world alone and uninformed. She was the one who had picked my parents, who had left me with my rings and the blue-bladed dagger I had yet to recover from Pyra. If anyone would have answers about my past, about the day of the attack, about what I was supposed to do, I felt it had to be her.

"I still don't like it," Ryder huffed. "There's no telling what kind of favor he'll cash in on."

"And that's a risk I knew I'd have to take." I suddenly felt tired. Tired of arguing. Tired of not knowing anything. Tired of the sleepless nights. "Me. Not you. Not Lachlan. Me. I'm not the reckless girl who charged at a Great Beast on the back of a kelpie with nothing but a spear to defend myself anymore."

In my periphery, Lach's hand shot into the air. He waved it around,

27

no doubt to ask a million questions about that nasty little fight in the desert, but I kept my attention on Ryder. "I am more informed now. I know what risks I have to take. This is one of them. If you say you're with me, then you'll have to trust me. And that means trusting my decisions about myself."

Ryder held my gaze for several beats before lowering his head, shoulders slumping in defeat. Lachlan whistled, low and slow, and knelt to pick up his knives, slipping them back up his sleeves. Even I felt a tingle of lightning shock up my spine. I hadn't expected Ryder to back down so quickly.

I didn't know if I liked it.

But that was something to consider later.

"Alright, we have a plan." I fidgeted with my sleeves. "We leave as soon as humanly possible. Let's send a promissory note to your contact about the oath and figure out how we're getting to this town that doesn't require using magic to fly." I sighed heavily. "If we've actually found Marinda, I need to think about how to approach this conversation. I can't do that if I'm worried about staying in the air."

"You got it, boss." Lachlan flipped his hat so its brim faced backward. "Me and my best buddy Ryder here got you covered."

Ryder grumbled, but followed us down the stairway to our tiny room to discuss strategy.

Chapter 5

I settled back, rubbing my hands over the worn velvet of the seat cushions, watching the color shift from periwinkle to navy back to periwinkle again. After a moment's hesitation, I allowed myself to relax and rock with the steady sway of the train streaking down the tracks. A few minutes later, I reached for the to-go cup of coffee I'd set on the matte silver table set between me and the seats I faced.

After another brief scuffle between Ryder and Lachlan over which mode of transportation was both the most direct and most efficient way to get to Romania, they'd settled on taking the train. Before boarding, I'd overheard Lachlan say something about surfing on top of one car and I shut that idea down, telling the elf under no uncertain terms was he to attempt anything that might freak people out. That was asking for a whole slew of problems I didn't want to deal with.

He'd agreed... but now I wondered why he'd agreed so quickly.

What was he up to?

I inhaled the scent of roasted beans and vanilla flavoring. I'd chosen this particular car because the only other inhabitant was a woman with more wrinkles than a rose sitting in the corner. She monitored a television tuned to an international news channel pinned to the wall on a mount.

A reporter stood outside of the United Nations buildings—I recognized the campus by now—motioning a lot with her hands, but

I couldn't understand the scrolling captioning at the bottom of the screen, so I looked away. The view outside my window was much more interesting, anyway, with its lush green fields and frosted mountain peaks in the distance.

The car bounced a bit, and I rolled my cup against my bottom lip. What did I want to find out from Marinda? More importantly, what did I need to know, and what did I most *want* to know? A golf ball-sized lump settled in my throat. I swallowed around it, thoughts whirling like a carousel.

I'd squared off against some of the most powerful beings on the planet without flinching, but the idea of talking to one witch set my nerves aflame. Go figure.

I took a gulp of coffee and nearly spat it back out when the voice of the Kraken slid softly through my thoughts. *Are you asking the right questions, Little One?* It asked.

Boundaries, I replied. *We've discussed this.*

I sensed the Great Beast waving a tentacle dismissively. *Boundaries mean nothing to me.*

Says the massive octopus confined to the water.

No need to get snippy, It said.

I have every reason to be snippy with you. I sank deeper into my seat. The hand that gripped the cup shook. I'd told the Beast who'd gifted me my powers to leave me alone two weeks ago when It had randomly popped up out of nowhere for the first time in months, addressing my thoughts while I showered. Our mental connection seemed to be strongest when I was touching water.

I'm still mad at you for abandoning me, I said. *You vanish when I lock Kaleal away and then come out of nowhere when she's back? No, I have nothing to say to you right now.*

The Kraken sighed deeply. *It's more complicated than you're making it out to be.*

No, it isn't. You could clear all this up pretty quickly if you'd just tell me what's going on.

The Kraken paused.

I loathed Its smooth way of talking, as if used to soothing bruised egos and straightening ruffled feathers. This wasn't a new demand of mine. It owed me answers, yet whenever I asked, the Kraken either changed the topic or melted away.

If I could explain, I would, It said. *But you must trust me when I say—*

The thing is, I don't *trust you.* My eyes darted to the television screen. People with cheery, fake smiles glugged filtered water in a commercial. *And I won't trust you until you give me the truth. Until you can do that much, I have nothing more to say to you.*

I severed our mental connection and slammed the cup on the table so hard the paper base crumpled. Light brown coffee spilled everywhere, though I stopped the rush of liquid before it dribbled over the edge. I evaporated the puddle with a thought, deciding to worry about the sticky residue it left behind later.

I still badly needed a caffeine fix.

My outburst must have startled the woman, because I felt her eyes on me. I didn't care. I had my allies, and I'd always counted the Kraken among them. But now I didn't trust the Beast's motives. I didn't understand Its allegiances. I definitely didn't trust Kaleal, and from where I stood, the timing of the Beast's actions aligned too closely with the comings and goings of my biggest enemy.

I rubbed at the spot on my table with my sleeve and tried to relax. If the Kraken wasn't ready to talk, there wasn't much I could do about it.

I'd barely cleared my thoughts when a pair of hands smacked the back of the seat on either side of my head. I whipped around, magic roaring in my blood as I prepared to either attack or defend, and found Lachlan looming over me. I slumped, powers retreating. A broad smile stretched across his face.

"Found you." He leaped over the table and dropped in the chair across from me, flinging one long leg over the arm comfortably. "I should have thought to check the most empty car first."

"It's like you don't know me at all," I murmured wryly.

Lachlan scanned the seats and nodded shortly, as if confirming something to himself. "Where did the Dark One go? I thought you two were joined by some invisible chain, the way Ryder hovers." The elf twisted in his chair again and sat up straight, bracing his elbows on his thighs. "I finally understand the phrase 'three's a crowd' because of him being all broody and judgmental all the time. I thought I'd have to hogtie and lock him in a closet if I wanted to talk to you alone ever again."

I propped a boot on the table and bobbled my knee. "You know he would escape by turning to smoke, right?"

Lachlan's lips puckered, then his expression cleared. "Not if I knocked him out first."

"I'd love to see that fight." I wished I hadn't knocked over my coffee, but going back to the car with food seemed like such a chore. "And he's not here right now because I asked for *space*. To think. About Marinda. Remember? Both of you were actually present for that conversation."

The elf hummed, tapped the back of his hand, shrugged. "I don't recall agreeing to that."

I entertained the idea of negating my earlier order banning actions that would garner too much attention in favor of tossing him out the window. He still had my Air magic, so he could fly back. But it might buy me a few minutes of peace and quiet. No. Probably shouldn't.

Instead, I settled for the diplomatic approach. "You said, with your hand over your heart, and I quote, 'I, Lachlan McAvoy, the cleverest elf to ever live, swear to give you, the boss, time to think by herself.' End quote. Tell me what about that isn't an agreement?"

"I recall saying nothing of the sort." The elf flung his ankle up on his thigh, lavender gaze intensifying as he plucked at his jacket. I was used to his constant twitching, but this was a bit much. "Besides, we need to talk."

I noted the touch of color in his cheekbones, the cap flipped backward, the stiff set to his shoulders, and promptly gave up all hope of weighing my thoughts before meeting Marinda. Some things were more important. Maybe Lach was finally ready to tell me what had him so bothered.

"Are we breaking up?" I asked, giving him room to retreat if he needed it. My phone vibrated, rattling the table. I flipped it over without looking at the screen.

"Sort of." He scratched his arm through his jacket. "After you get settled in Romania, I need to break away for a bit."

The knots in my chest relaxed. I'd suspected as much, given his twitchiness and erratic behavior of late. My adrenaline-junkie friend wasn't built for long stretches without adventure. "I understand."

His foot slipped from his knee and hit the thin carpet with a thud. He leaned across the table, crowding me. "You do?"

I poked his chest with my index finger, nudging him back. "Lach, come on, I know you. Well, I know enough *about* you to know what we're doing right now isn't up your alley." I tugged one of my feet up and settled it under my thigh. The buckles dug into my leg uncomfortably. "I don't expect things to get much more thrilling once we find Marinda, either. When we first met, you said you hunted the thrill of excitement and danger. What we're doing now is neither of those."

Lach sagged in his seat. He peered out the window as we passed a field with wooden fences penning in fluffy, white sheep. My phone vibrated again.

"That's a relief," he said. "Not that watching this weird power play, sexual tension thing between you and the incubus isn't fun, but... I'm glad you understand." Lach rubbed his arm in the same spot as before.

"I wasn't sure if you'd be so understanding since you offered the oath and all."

A knot pulled tight in my gut. "What are you talking about?"

Oath? I'd never offered Lachlan an oath. I tried to recall our conversations, wondering where I might have messed up. The elf retreated to his side of the table again, lips pressed firmly together, forearm crushed to his chest as if realizing he'd said too much.

My phone buzzed again.

"Should you get that?" Lachlan asked.

I shook my head sharply. Whatever it was could wait. "What oath are you talking about?"

Lach wasn't built for evasiveness. He liked to dabble in secrets but wasn't particularly great at keeping them when pressed.

"Fine." He ran his free hand over his hat and rolled his sleeve up as he extended his arm. Below his wrist, across the serpentine curve of his artery, a water crest tattoo was etched into his skin. Unlike most I'd seen, this was only an outline. I traced the edge with my nail. Goosebumps dotted his pale skin, and tiny ripples of blue fanned out along the darkened lines.

"I don't understand," I breathed. "This isn't like the other oaths." I gripped my own arm, circling the wrist decorated with three black bands. "What is this? How did this happen?"

"You offered me a place in your court, boss."

My gaze jerked up to his, the conversation in the kitchen of the Bellagio suite screaming through my mind. I'd told him my home was his—should he ever need one. Was that all it took? A statement as vague as that could open up a spot for someone as a member of my theoretical court? I almost laughed. What kind of court would that look like, anyway? And where would I rule—*who* would I rule? I'd finally made the connection of being some sort of queen, but queen of what? And who cared?

I sensed the whirlwind that was Kaleal stirring and shut her down, not needing to hear her jabs about how I needed to take my future—and my place in it—more seriously.

Lach's lips twitched, and I got the sense he was trying to not laugh at the pained shock on my face.

"It hasn't filled in because I haven't decided if I'll accept your offer," he explained. "But it's there. An opportunity to stand beside you, anyway—an offer no God has extended to any elves in thousands of years." He cuffed my shoulder lightly. "Figures you'd be the one to break the mold."

His gesture, the casual fluidity of it, eased the anxiety rising in my chest. Whatever happened, however it happened, it would work out. It had to.

"That's a shame for the other Gods, now, isn't it?" I kept my tone light, aiming for levity. "I think your skills come in handy most of the time, and you keep Ryder on his toes."

I clasped my hands. "But I'll miss you—when you're gone. Against all odds, you've grown on me."

"My fungal qualities are often unappreciated," he mused.

I pulled my braid over my shoulder, ran the fuzzy tip over my fingers. "Lach, I don't care about the oaths or what I've said or haven't said. I will not force you to stand by my side or anything. You've got stuff to do, volcanos to walk across on tightropes, centaur-infested forests to clear—" Lachlan's grin practically engulfed his face. "Whatever it is you do when you're not confined to Cogscraig."

"Coolest boss ever," he said as my phone buzzed again. He picked it up, held it out. "Are you sure you don't need to get that?"

A burst of red caught my attention, and I glanced at the television in the corner, at the frantic stream of words crossing the screen, the rounded eyes of the reporter as she tried to stop people spilling from the building behind her, microphone extended. Though my ability to translate languages still hadn't kicked in, I knew in my gut something was wrong.

I snatched the phone from Lach as the screen lit up again.

Finn.

He never called, only texted. My stomach hollowed, and I stood, energy snapping through me too violently to remain sitting.

"Go find him," I ordered Lachlan. He knew who I meant and for once didn't drop a wise-ass remark about the incubus. He pushed through the door joining the cars as I brought the phone to my ear. "What's happened?"

"You need to get to Rome. Now," my guardian ordered tersely.

On TV, people sprinted down the street. The close-captioned words unraveled before my eyes as Finn uttered the very words every person on the planet—human and fey—feared most.

"Nuclear talks failed, Z. The United Nations is splintering. The big guys have locked in their alliance and are threatening total annihilation if they don't get cooperation from the rest of the world by the end of the week." Finn paused, and I heard the drone of what sounded like a news program in the background. I paced the length of the aisle to the door and back again, vision blurring as thoughts zipped through my head.

"The U.S., U.K., France—they're all retreating, working to get their experimental shields running before time runs out," Finn said. The door to our railcar slid open. Ryder and Lachlan emerged, eyes bright with urgency.

In my ear, Finn continued, "The little guys are trying to form pacts—I don't know. It's one giant cluster. We're calling everyone back to Order HQ while we figure this out. Oron and Pyra left the moment the U.N. dissolved. They'll be here later today." The strain in his voice nearly shattered me. "We need you here, Z. We need you here yesterday."

My braid still dangled over my shoulder, and I dug my fingers into the loops. I hadn't found Marinda. I hadn't gotten the answers I needed. But I *had* promised Joseph and Finn I'd come if they needed my help. And if I didn't get there now… who knew what world we'd be left with.

If a world would be left at all.

I held Ryder's eyes first, then Lach's, silently rallying them for battle. "I'm already on my way."

Chapter 6

Despite the conversation we'd finished, the newest development in my life was all the encouragement Lach needed to suction cup himself to my side. The end of the world, I supposed, affected everyone differently.

I'd wanted to make it to the outskirts of Rome where the Order Headquarters was located within a day. However, Ryder argued a straight shot from the eastern half of Romania with three fey flying at their fastest speeds required an enormous amount of energy. At his urging, and when I'd reached the limits of my mental control over Air, we'd crashed at a hotel the incubus scrounged up in some middle-sized Croatian city I couldn't pronounce.

A dreamless slumber, and twelve hours later, we blearily woke up and continued onward.

Now, here we stood, at the mouth of a canyon I eyed with heavy distrust. The last time I'd stared down that rocky, dusty trail, I'd had the might of three other Gods at my back. We had been prepared to die to stop the destructive nature of the Order under Geoffrey's command. Now I faced a similar, yet exceedingly worse situation.

"It's a path," Lachlan said. He finger-combed knots from his hair, styling his wavy locks into a semblance of sweaty tidiness, only to smash his hat down on top of it. "Dirt, rock, brown plants of some kind, a whole lot of red dust. A path."

"It's more than that." Ryder stretched, stiff from the flight. Stork-like, he balanced on one leg as he stretched his thigh muscles then switched to take care of the other side. "It's the end of one chapter and the start of another. Zara's self-proclaimed freedom ends the moment she walks down that path."

"It's going to be like that, huh?" Lach bounced on the balls of his feet, threw a few fake punches. "Pretty metaphors? Fluttery language? I didn't think you ran that deep."

Ryder smirked. "I'll have you know, some of the most esteemed poets in literary history were daemoni. Our kind are more than sexual deviants with beautiful faces stereotyped by jealous bigots. We have—"

"Nope, not daemoni." Lachlan extended his long arm, pointer finger extended. "You. Only you."

Dark mist cascaded down Ryder's legs, overtaking the path, obscuring our bags propped against a rock. "You're gonna wish you were—"

"Enough. Both of you." I shoved them apart with some air currents. I understood why Lachlan was so entertained by goading Ryder. While complex in his own ways, the elf's elementary-level amusement was a simple thing. But why Ryder allowed himself to be so easily manipulated was a mystery to me. As a reformed prince of darkness who'd built a multi-billion dollar empire from nothing, he should know better. "Both of you are wrong."

Lach stuck his tongue out at the incubus and dove for his bag. He pulled out two homemade granola bars and tossed one at me. Ryder's chest expanded, the veins bulging in his neck, before he released his breath.

"Then why are you so apprehensive?" Ryder asked.

I swapped the food for the phone in my back pocket and checked the text messages. Yep, this was the right spot. Joseph had told me to avoid both the main gates and the port along the river. People seeking sanctuary inside the Order's walls had gathered there. Instead, he'd directed me to the only remaining opening in the magical dome protecting the campus.

This entrance to the south, tucked in among large, rolling hills.

I shoved my phone into my bag and slapped my hand over the sheath at my thigh, checking for the silver dagger I'd strapped into place upon landing. I glanced at Ryder. "Last time I was here, things didn't go so well for me. I'd rather not see history repeat itself."

Ryder scoffed. "The odds of that happening are slim. I doubt a legion of soldiers is on the other side preparing to cut you into a million pieces this time."

I grimaced. "But there are several billion people living in several hundred nations all freaking out about a dozen hotheads who may or may not decide to push little red buttons and send this planet into a new ice age."

The incubus canted his head. "I don't think that's how nuclear fallout works."

"Oh, right." I shouldered my bag and tightened the straps around my shoulders. "I forgot you've got first-hand experience dealing with the unique catastrophe that comes after dozens of nuclear weapons detonate all at once, decimating everything and everyone.

"Wait—" I lifted on my toes and jabbed him below the sternum. "No, I must be thinking of someone else."

The swirling of his dark eyes stilled and his lips quirked.

"No response? Good. Glad you see things my way." I swiveled on my heel and marched down the trail, gravel crunching underfoot. Within seconds, thick, red dust coated my boots and jeans. "Now, let's go."

As I led the way, eyes fixed straight ahead, I swore I heard Ryder chuckle and murmur, "That's my girl," but the canyon could have been playing tricks on me. I did hear Lachlan rush to catch up, begging to hear more about the story Ryder had hinted at earlier. The one that ended with an explosion involving me, a glass wall, and a man who'd wanted me dead at the time.

A man who *still* wanted me dead?

I hadn't given it much thought about it, but Joseph had ordered Geoffrey be imprisoned at headquarters. There wasn't any better place to keep him both securely locked away and protected against the outside world. The former Hand of the Gods had made his fair share of enemies that stretched beyond the Gods themselves.

I wondered how Geoffrey had changed over the past few months. Was magic really to blame for his insanity? Could my decision to save him have changed his worldview again?

If the truth whispered to me by the cursed longbow Lachlan kept rolled in his jacket was correct, then Geoffrey's mind had changed in a big way once before.

Maybe it wouldn't be so bad for history to strike twice.

Our little group kept conversation to a minimum as we trudged through the narrow pass. While Lachlan occasionally grumbled about the lack of scenery and giant boulders to scale, I didn't mind the walk. It felt good to stretch my legs after all that flying. I understood how to use the Air magic, but flying still made me nervous sometimes. It felt too much like willingly placing myself in the hands of fate.

Before I was ready, the iron arches of the Order gates cut into the sides of the cliffs before us, fierce metal defenders barricading our way into the city. They appeared to be the same gates Oron had ripped from the sides of the canyon and dropped to the ground our first go-around. I wondered if the Earth God had put them back in place.

The monstrosities stretched two stories high and perched flat against the ground where someone had laid flat stones to ease the process of opening and closing them. Emblazoned on their surfaces were patterns of half-moon Dragon scales and sleek Thunderbird feathers. Curved fangs belonging to the Ramalia bracketed the long crack dividing the two doors. A pair of black eyes watched carefully above them as the reaching tentacles of the Kraken wound around the edges of the gates, searching for a way in—or out.

Lachlan whistled, low and slow, one thumb hooked in the strap of his bag. "The Order does nothing by halves, does it?"

"Never." I held up my hand, squinting against the harsh rays of the sun blasting between the spires adorning the top of the barricade. "And why should they, when they have the Gods on their side?"

"That's a conceited way of looking at things," Lach grumbled.

"What happened to the outpost?" Ryder pointed at the cliff where a glass observation tower had stood before. The building had been cleared away, with trees and brush already overtaking the flat, empty space left behind. "How are we supposed to get inside? Do your powers open it or something?"

"That's a good question." I fired off a text to Joseph asking that very thing, and clicked my tongue against the roof of my mouth when he didn't reply after a minute or two. I tried calling him, then Finn, but both went straight to voicemail. "They must be busy."

Lach propped a foot on a small rock and untied his laces. "I wonder what they might be busy with. Is anything big going on right now?" He twisted the strings into a neat bow and patted them cheekily.

My eyes lifted skyward. "Weren't you supposed to be off riding polar bears in Antarctica right about now?"

"First off, polar bears don't live in Antarctica, so that would be weird." The elf brushed dust from his shirt. "And second: No, things, again, got infinitely more interesting with you around. I'm picking up on a trend."

"Ignore him." Ryder pressed his hand to the small of my back. Heat coiled around the base of my spine. It felt like the times I'd looked down from the tallest diving board, measuring my heartbeats as I prepared to jump into the chlorinated water beckoning below. I'd never competed in diving, but I'd always loved the sharp sense of anticipation that came with it. "Work your magic, glowstick."

He was right. I tugged on the collar of my jacket, shrugged the feeling aside, and approached the gates. Hormones were the last thing I needed to think about right now. Relationships were an unnecessary complication. So what he was darkly handsome with a dimple that curved his smile in a stupidly sexy way? And who cared he couldn't seem to get enough of me when I was around, yet respected my need for independence?

And he could be yours and yours alone.

The errant thought fluttered away so quickly I wasn't sure I'd recognized it. Had that been *my* thought? It hadn't felt like me... but it certainly couldn't have been Kaleal. She did not try to disguise her bias against Ryder, and I couldn't imagine her using that dislike as a front to deeper emotion. I wasn't sure she was capable of feeling something like love, not with the way she manipulated everyone and everything around her.

"Are you praying for the gates to open?" Lachlan called. "I don't think it works like that since you're the God who would hear said prayers and... you're also standing right there to answer them."

I blinked. The metallic scent of the gates filled my nose. They radiated a heat that reminded me of the flames burning in my belly. Every few seconds, speckles of gold flickered around the edges of the feathers and the Kraken's tentacles seemed to sway. How strange little details like those would become evident at close proximity. I needed to ask Joseph if the Gods had crafted these gates, maybe infused their magic into them.

With a shrug, I pressed my palm against the metal, biting back a gasp at the sharp chill that sliced through my skin. The cold battled brutally with the boiling heat roiling inside me as my magic reacted to the forces that seemingly warred against me, trying to figure out who and what I was. Sweat beaded along my hairline. I bit into my lower

43

lip so deeply I tasted copper on my tongue. Despite that, I pushed, shoving my magic deeper into the metal.

At first, the gates resisted, diverting my magic from their inner depths. But the longer I held my ground, the more my magic coiled with that intertwined in the gate. Reds, blues, and greens flashed across the dark gray surface, shifting faster and faster, matching the pace of the magic I fed into it.

It stopped as abruptly as it started.

A low, slow grumble shook my bones, and I stumbled back on watery knees, believing the lock barring the gates had lifted. Yet when I pushed, the doors held fast.

"Zara," Ryder called. I ignored him and the warning in his tone.

Another rumble rattled through me. Small rocks danced along the base of the gates. I frowned, nearly crouched to examine them, then stopped when dry heat, hot as the midday sun in the desert, wafted over me, fanning the tiny hairs that refused to stay bound in my braid.

Another rumble.

My jaw flexed, hands fisted.

I tipped my head straight back and peered up into the burning gaze of a dragon.

Chapter 7

Bronze whiskers thick as shoestrings flared haphazardly around Its muzzle, fluttering in time with the Beast's long, slow breathing. A mosaic of scales ranging from the softest shades of rose to the deepest tone of merlot shimmered in the sunlight, offset only by the Dragon's gleaming shamrock eyes. The scales deepened to black around Its curved front claws, which the Beast hooked around a pair of spikes at the top of the gate. Its body draped in folds across the top of the iron bars, long enough to stretch the length of an Olympic-sized swimming pool, occasionally flashing a ripple of leathery skin that ran the length of Its back.

So this was the Great Beast of Fire.

No one in, no one out. The Beast's internal dialogue boomed inside my thoughts, ricocheting around my skull, brash and bold as the creature itself. Kaleal unraveled herself from the mists inside which she slept. Exactly what I didn't need right now.

I took one careful step back, then another, telling myself it wasn't so much a retreat as a strategic realignment. The farther I moved, the more my awareness of my surroundings spread. Though weirdly faint, it occurred to me Ryder was shouting at me, calling me away from the creature.

Not yet.

"I need to get inside. I'm expected," I said. The Great Beasts I'd met so far were proud, regal creatures whose very presence demanded respect. I brought my hands up, fingers splayed, back arched slightly. "You must know who I am. I don't doubt you can sense my magic, so please let me and my friends pass."

Talons screeched across the face of the gate, digging inch-deep grooves in the intricately carved designs as the Dragon repositioned Itself higher. It didn't have wings, but a thick flap of skin curved around the circumference of Its neck, flexing as the Beast stared me down.

Sha has orders, It drawled. *They don't include bowing to abominations.*

"That's rude." I straightened, abandoning all signs of deference. Seriously, what was Its deal? And was It really talking in the third person?

"Don't tell me you can talk to that thing." Lachlan appeared on my left, TruthTeller strung, invisible arrow drawn between two gloved fingers. He'd flipped his cap backward, his bag nowhere in sight. "Cuz if you are, I'm starting to doubt there's anything you can't do."

"I—"

Good luck with her, Kaleal chimed in, cutting off my reply which came at the same time Ryder grumbled something from my right. The cacophony of voices threw off my spatial awareness, confusing me. I closed my eyes, trying to focus on the Original God, wondering if she'd have anything of value to relay. *Sha never listens to anyone she doesn't like.*

Let me guess, she doesn't like me, I said to Kaleal.

You do seem to bring out the worst in others. You may consider getting that professionally checked out someday. Kaleal settled in behind my eyes, intrigue coloring her tone. *I'm interested to see how you weasel your way out of this one.*

Lovely. She wasn't going to be helpful, just her normal brand of irritating. I opened my eyes again. The Great Beast had hefted more of her body to the top of the gate. Her winding tail shot with shimmers of yellows and golds curled around the farthest-most stake.

"Please." I struggled for patience. "Please let us through. I'll get Pyra and she can clear up this whole thing."

Such amusing thoughts. The flame of her tongue flickered along her burnt-black lips. *The Fire God commanded Sha to guard this gate. Sha is all too happy to comply.*

I rubbed my neck and glanced at Ryder. He'd shifted into his second skin, wings spread, muscles dark and hard as obsidian. "She's not going to let us through."

His lips thinned. "You want to go back?"

"I'd rather not fight the core of Fire if I don't have to." This could not be happening at a worse time. I was already running late, and now I couldn't get in.

"You're no fun." Lachlan lowered his bow but kept his arrow drawn. "Going back will take *forever*. It's not like we can fly. You told us yourself, Joseph had them extend the magical barricade. It will take the better part of the day to circle back around."

He had a point. A ripple of amusement flared from Kaleal, but I couldn't focus on her. My attention was already divided a dozen ways to Sunday.

She thinks she can go. The Dragon leaped from the gate, body flowing with the grace of a ribbon to the ground, where she crouched on stumpy legs the size of propane tanks. *She does not know the rules.*

"Rules?" I asked. Lachlan jerked TruthTeller back up, polished wood creaking as he cranked back the invisible string. I cracked my knuckles and summoned my magic. Between Water and Air, I should have an edge. I wouldn't unleash the flames licking at the base of my spine yet. What was the point?

She who challenges Sha must stand behind her words. The Beast's mouth gaped wide, revealing double sets of shimmering jade teeth.

No, I definitely did not have time for this. I didn't remember challenging her, but if the Beast wouldn't let me go without a fight, then at least one decision was already made for me. I lifted a sword of ice, tip pointed at the creature. "If my friends and I beat you, you'll let us pass?"

Of course. Putrid breath washed across us as Sha laughed silently. *Not that it will happen.*

I totally took that as a yes.

The earth groaned painfully, a bubble beneath it expanding—and burst, showering us with water as the geyser erupted.

At my side, Lachlan released a magical arrow, barely flinching at the truth it fired back at him, and sprinted away. The bolt hit the Beast in the center of the chest, and she stumbled back, unleashing a roar that brought boulders tumbling down the sides of the cliff. Ryder launched into the sky, smoke uncurling from his fists, as I hopped onto the third fountain of water shooting from the crack I'd created.

I shouted a warning, watching with icy horror when a boulder nearly hit Lach as he rounded the creature, but the elf dodged in time. That was far too close.

The elf fired again, and the Dragon pounced at him, jaw stretched wide, sensing easy prey. But my friend wasn't one to underestimate. He drew back a fist and launched it forward, releasing a sonic boom of power that hit the Beast square between the eyes. The Dragon hovered a moment, dazed, flattening to the ground as Sha reevaluated the elf who whipped his bow up.

Sha didn't have time to consider him long, because Ryder shouted, releasing a dark, blanketing mist I knew contained the forgotten dregs of night terrors and other haunted things. The nightmare hounds tripped over one another, baying loudly with their eagerness to terrify.

Would that work against one of the Great Beasts? Did they dream?

The curling wisps of thick fog obscured the Dragon and the ground, which I used to my advantage. Puffy black clouds billowed from the east, moving in from the sea, answering my call. Who needed Fire anyway, when Water was at such ready supply?

For a few terse moments, the Dragon went quiet. I wondered if Ryder had pulled off something incredible, until a loud, humming sound rattled through me, like a laser powering up.

… that's annoying…

The blackness exploded like a star erupting in the Milky Way. The violent blast of light blinded and deafened me, knocking me clean off my tower. I flailed, lost in a field of never-ending white when Air rushed to my aid. I smacked into the pane of hardened molecules with a crack that nearly shattered my elbow, knocking the wind from my lungs. I gagged, curling inward, gasping for the oxygen that had abandoned me.

I coughed, beating at my chest, kneeling in mid-air, blinking and shuddering when I realized the world had gone dark again, a complete absence of light. How could the Dragon of Fire create such complete and utter—

Lachlan.

He'd pulled a fast one with his lingering control over Air, using a favorite trick of mine to create a blackout. I wondered how far the darkness stretched. It would have taken an incredible amount of energy to expand a field this wide and unconfined. It wouldn't last long.

And it didn't.

Two more blinks and the darkness faded. Beneath me, the Dragon paced the floor of the canyon, spinning in a series of endless circles. The stripe down her back illuminated, a living cape of flame. The Beast must have sensed me because Sha whipped around, tail lashing, smashing boulders to rubble.

"Had enough?" I rose to one knee.

Steam rose from her scales. *Sha never surrenders.*

Steam.

Wait a minute. Droplets from my geysers hissed when they touched the Beast's scales. When Sha used her powers... she had to draw on Fire. And what put out Fire better than...

Water.

I ripped down a volley of hailstones, pelting the Beast as a burst of wicked-hot flames erupted from her mouth. I narrowly jumped from my panel before the fire reached me and coasted smoothly to the ground. Ryder dive-bombed Sha's head, darting at the creature's eyes, distracting her as Lachlan approached from the back. My chest squeezed tight when the incubus barely avoided a burst of flame.

Wasting no more time, I raced to Lachlan's side and grabbed his hand. Electricity coursed between us. Forked lightning, hot and vibrant, shot from our bodies, slamming into the creature's hide. Sha roared, the flames streaking down her spine momentarily dimming to the might of our electrical current, but the Dragon rallied and the flames sprouted taller and wider than ever before.

Sha roared again. The strange humming from before—the kind that had nearly turned my insides to jelly—started up again. I shoved Lachlan, recognizing the sound for what it was, and dove behind one of the ten-foot-wide boulders, shielding my eyes in the crook of my arm as the Dragon went total neutron star blast for a second time. I smelled burning hair. Electricity coursed madly across my skin, the tiny hairs on my arms standing on end, reacting to whatever the Beast had done.

Claws scraped heavily, and I peered out from behind my arm. The Beast had jumped on top of what remained of our protective rock and glared down at us, talons curled, chest heaving. Sha glowed, bright and brilliant as an ember.

Sha never loses.

"So you think." I grinned crazily and Sha cocked her head, a strange look crossing her scaled face. I truly hated to extinguish something so beautiful. Power rocked through me. Thunder roared. I was about to rain literal floods down upon our shoulders.

"Stop. All of you, stop. Hold up one stinking second."

My mind blanked.

Pyra?

"Zara, don't you dare do what I know you're about to do," she warned. "If you do, I'll rip your arms from your body and beat you bloody with them."

The Fire God's shout cut through me like a blast of arctic wind. I lost the thread tying me to the boiling black clouds overhead, and I twisted wildly, searching for the pint-size person. Her stop sign-red pixie cut bobbed around the rocks crumbled near the gate, its doors flung wide.

"Me?" I waved dramatically at the Dragon, which lay sprawled across the boulder, monster head resting on her paws, docile as a house cat. "What about that thing? She tried to blast us apart twice with that weird light deal."

"Sha is a Dragon. You're a God. But, honestly, you're all a bunch of heathens." Pyra choked on something and spat loudly. I'd lost sight of her in the rubble and red dust. "I swear, I can't take any of you anywhere without you trying to drown someone or blast them to bits with—yes, Sha, I'm talking about you."

That was only one time, Sha rumbled. Gone was the creature intent on my destruction. Now she peered down at me with suspicious innocence. I almost imagined her batting nonexistent lashes. I inclined my head, eyes narrowing, careful to keep the Beast in my line of vision.

Ryder dropped lightly in front of me, wings pulled tight against his back as Pyra darted around a giant hole in the ground. For the life of me, I couldn't remember how it had gotten there. "Pyra," he drawled in greeting, folding his arms across his chest.

"Will you explain what's going on?" I demanded of the God.

Pyra ignored me and batted at the incubus as she dipped around him, picking up speed. "Outta the way, Gloomy. I've seen enough of your dour face to last two lifetimes. My girl is finally back and I won't have you spoiling this moment."

I barely got my arms spread in time for her to crash into me with the power of a bullet train. I wheezed, stumbling back as Pyra wrapped tight around me, practically scaling my body like a not-so-fuzzy koala.

"Good to see you, too," I gasped.

"Don't give me that." Her voice was muffled against my jacket. "I know you didn't think of me once while you were out stopping curses, saving fey, changing the course of the world, all that jazz."

"Now that's not true." I awkwardly patted the back of her head, shaking my head at Ryder, who clucked his tongue at a charred hole he'd discovered in his sleeve. Lachlan had popped up out of nowhere and leaned against one of the canyon walls, casually rolling TruthTeller into a ball—a magical ability of the weapon I didn't understand. "I thought of you plenty. Besides, you, Oron, and Joseph were doing the real heavy lifting. Taking on the Order and dealing with the impending nuclear war—"

"You mean *failing* to stop an impending nuclear war." Pyra released me as suddenly as she'd grabbed me and patted her pockets absently. She still wore the same uniform: black cotton on black leather with black boots to finish the look. Sunlight refracted off the edges of the throwing stars sewn into her belt. "But considering our failure is what it took to bring you home, maybe it's not entirely a bad thing."

Lachlan chuckled. I cleared my throat. "Speaking of the nuclear talks—"

"Found it," Pyra chirped. She withdrew a raspberry Dum Dum from inside her vest, unwrapped it, and shoved it in her mouth. The white stick bobbed a few times as she rolled it around her teeth. "I'm cutting back on the cigs."

"And by that, she means she's down to a pack a day," Ryder intoned.

Pyra turned to him, rubbing her brow with her middle finger. "Who invited you, anyway?"

The incubus rolled his eyes and looked around the ruins of our makeshift battlefield, keeping his body slightly angled toward Sha.

Pyra pulled the sucker from her mouth with a pop and waved it at me. "What's with you and this gate? Did it do something to you? I mean, it only took Oron about five seconds to get it upright after last time, but this…" She scanned the mayhem of what remained of the canyon. "You may have outdone yourself with this one."

I clapped my hands. "Yes. Speaking of. What's with the Dragon?"

Pyra's tongue darted out to lick her sugary treat. "About that…"

"Yes?"

Her lips pursed. "Joseph didn't tell me you'd be coming in this way."

"And? That gives Sha permission to kill me?" Steam had stopped wafting from the Beast's scales. Sha had closed her eyes, but I knew she wasn't asleep.

Pyra's shoulder lifted. "I did tell her to keep the crazies out."

My mouth opened and closed a few times. I had no words. None.

She patted my arm. "You've missed out on a lot. Most people are fixated on getting through the main gates, which is all fine and good. The Order has those on lockdown, anyway. They're also prepared to lower the barrier if it comes down to it." Pyra shoved the sucker into her mouth and spoke around it. "But a few figured out where this entrance was and it's caused some issues. Sha's been monitoring it for us since she has nothing better to do."

"I see." And I did, but something about the Beast's attitude felt off somehow.

Pyra crunched down on the hard candy with a sound that made my teeth ache, and tucked the stick into a pouch at her belt, one she'd reserved for cigarette butts in the past. "Granted, Sha's been taking her job a bit too seriously these days. But now that you're here and—"

Pyra glanced over me quickly— "*mostly* in one piece, no harm, no foul. She's pretty chill when you get to know her. Come on, let's get going. We're late for the meeting."

Pyra tugged on my hand, guiding me toward the Order compound, but I met the Great Beast's eyes before we vanished inside, noted the sharp gleam within them. No, between that and Kaleal's not-so-quiet chuckle, something told me Sha and I would never reach the 'pretty chill' phase of our relationship.

Chapter 8

"It's about time you showed up." Pyra signaled to some soldiers gathered inside the gate and motioned for them to close the doors. One of them reached immediately for one of the large handles, but the others seemed thunderstruck by the destruction we left outside, mouths wide and arms crossed. "Earth's guys were already here. I swear, Seth hasn't left since we overthrew the old regime. It's rare to see Joseph without that dung beetle at his elbow." Her nose wrinkled.

"Xi—the High Priest of my temple—tagged along with Oron and me. He was helping us in Geneva when everything blew up." She mimed an explosion with her hands. "We got here this morning. Joseph's been pacing nonstop since then. If anyone needs to try meditation, it's him. That guy is steeped in stress. It isn't healthy. Anyway, because he's so wigged out, demanding we do something, I thought for a hot minute they'd try to hold a vote without you here."

"What stopped them?" I asked.

Black steel buildings with polished glass windows rose around us, growing taller and thinner the deeper we walked into the city. I wondered what they housed, given their industrial feel. I hadn't examined the architecture too closely the last time I'd been here; I'd been far too focused on getting out to see much of anything else. A black Sprinter van passed us on the freshly paved streets, its windows too darkly tinted for me to see inside. My head turned as it went, following its path, unable to shake the feeling I was being watched.

"A bunch of paperwork mostly," Pyra said. "The new council members are sticklers for paperwork. I mean, that doesn't surprise me, given who appointed them, but even Joseph has his limits. His face turned so red when one of them told him he needed to fill out a form for extra supplies in triplicate." The Fire God chuckled, patting her cheeks. "But he didn't yell. He never does. He's trying to instill a sense of decorum of whatever he prattles on about all the time."

A man in camouflage fatigues and shiny black boots approached on the sidewalk. When he drew close, he stopped, saluting us with a stiff arm, heels snug together. Pyra sighed and tapped two fingers to her temple before trailing off in a wave that passed before her face.

The soldier waited for us all to move by before he dropped his arm.

"See what I mean?" Pyra murmured. She tugged another sucker from her pocket and tapped its blue-raspberry head against her palm. "Even my temple doesn't require stuff like saluting superiors on the street. I asked to get rid of it, but *no*." She drew out the vowel as she popped the sucker in her mouth. "Something like that required filling out a stack of forms longer than my forearm."

My phone buzzed in my pocket. I pulled it out, flipped open the screen, and frowned. Now Joseph got back to me? His message was terse: *Where are you?*

My fingers flew over the keypad, letting him know we were crossing the compound now.

Metal clanged to my right and Lachlan held up his hands across the street as garbage spilled from a trashcan. He batted away my questioning look and trotted to rejoin our group. I considered asking what he was up to, then let it go. Some things were better left alone.

Ryder snagged my sleeve, and I realized Pyra had swung a hard right. He motioned to my phone. "What was that?"

"Joseph," I replied as my phone buzzed again.

The screen flashed with a new message: *You were supposed to be here eight hours ago. Stop dawdling and hurry up.*

I must have made a sound, because Ryder dragged me to a stop. Pyra noticed we were no longer following and backtracked, her eyes flicking between us. I snapped the device closed without replying. "He's being weird," I told Ryder.

"How so?"

"I don't know what his deal is. He sounds peeved, ordering me to hurry like he's my boss or something." I shoved my phone into my back pocket harder than I needed to. "We needed to get some sleep, or we would have passed out mid-flight. And he's the one who didn't answer when I tried asking him about the gate—" I rounded on Pyra. "Were there any new developments in the nuclear crisis over the past hour?"

She shook her head. "Not that I'm aware of." She pointed her thumb down the street. "We're almost there. It's about a block down. The campus has expanded a ton since Joseph took over. It's a pain to get around, but it's handy having all our primary resources in one place."

Ryder grunted and folded my hand in his, urging me along. "There's stressed, and then there are unrealistic expectations. He should recognize the difference."

"He should." The Fire God snapped her fingers. The black tape around her middle finger and thumb sparked a small flame that she squeezed. "But I also think you should cut him a little slack. I don't think the guy sleeps most of the time, he's so busy."

Our pace was markedly faster, and conversation all but died out. I scanned the street, the buildings, the rooftops, noting the soldiers stationed uniformly on the corners, semi-automatic rifles strapped across their chests. They, too, wore green instead of the black I'd grown accustomed to under Geoffrey's reign. I wondered if that had been a deliberate decision on Joseph's part.

57

And beyond the soldiers at the end of the block… I stuttered to a halt, my insides turning glacial.

A spire that competed with the Eiffel Tower for height and the Burj Khalifa in intimidation loomed high above the small city. Matchstick scaffolding wrapped around its top, and a few blurry figures shifted around on it. They'd reconstructed the top story I'd detonated in a desperate attempt to keep the former Hand of the Gods from shoving a knife through my heart, but the roof still wasn't finished.

"We're not going there, are we?" I didn't recognize my own voice—the meek squeak it was.

Pyra followed my gaze and shook her head, expression smoothing. "No. Seth wanted to, though. The top floor is where they used to hold meetings of this magnitude or some nonsense like that."

She quickly diverted us from the tower, directing us west, and we emerged at some sort of open square space with a fountain of white stones in the middle. The plaza was ringed with buildings marked with official-sounding plaques I didn't recognize.

A lot more had changed in my absence than I'd expected.

"But the noise from the construction is too loud," Pyra said, still talking about the tower. "And Joseph wants to get that project done so it's out of the way. They settled on meeting at the legal center right over there instead."

I didn't follow the finger she extended, showing the way. My mind was still back in that room. The room with the four crests of the four Gods cut into the walls, the crests with eternal flames that once burned on rounded pieces of colored glass. Flames Geoffrey had extinguished in an effort to douse me and my friends forever. The room I'd destroyed not once but twice, fully believing I'd escaped one quick death only to embrace another, slower version. The room in which I'd also decided to keep my most despised enemy alive, despite everything he'd done to me and to the world.

I wondered where they kept Geoffrey now.

"Hey, Zara, you're going the wrong way." Pyra's call stopped me alongside the fountain and she jogged to catch up. Lachlan and Ryder hung back, arms crossed, matching frowns marring their faces. They would hate to know how similar they looked right now.

Pyra squinted up at me, nodding grimly. "Are you ok? Seriously, don't worry about Joseph, he's juggling a million things right now—most of which we'll never know about. After this meeting, you guys can talk. He'll be in a better place, regardless, once this vote is out of the way." She rubbed her nose and smiled hesitantly. "He'll finally be able to feed the sharks something for their news cycle."

"Yeah, I guess." I didn't like the roiling in my stomach, the unease that settled beneath my skin like the feeling of drinking too much caffeine too fast. Jittery. That was the last thing I wanted to feel before meeting with the other Gods and leaders from the various temples to make the most important decision of my entire existence. "I'll be fine."

Pyra shook her head. "Yeah, you look real fine right now. If pale and sickly is fine." She reached into her jacket and fumbled around. "Here, maybe this will help you feel better."

She held out a sheathed dagger. My heart elevated to my throat as she presented it to me, a sliver of its blue-tinted steel visible between the hilt and the top of the sheath. "I believe this belongs to you."

Nerves fluttering, I reached out, relaxing when I wrapped my hand around the handle, uncaring of the curious expressions of people crossing the plaza. The weapon fit perfectly in my hand. I passed the sheath back to Pyra, who squirreled it away once more, and I spun the blade a few times, admiring the flicker of the metal, the dance of the light that bounced off it.

"I knew that would work." The embers in Pyra's scarlet eyes flared with approval.

Along with two silver rings in the shape of the water crest I wore on a necklace, this dagger was the only thing my temple had left with me as a baby. I had yet to unearth the meaning behind both artifacts, but they were *mine*—a claim I couldn't make about anything else, since the Order burned my childhood home to the ground.

I'd left the weapon with Pyra when she'd confronted me about leaving Geneva and backing away from our quest to stop nuclear warfare. She had refused to let me go without some assurance I'd return. Now, months later, I removed the silver dagger I'd bought as a temporary replacement, wrapped the new thigh sheath around my leg, and stuck my rightful weapon inside.

It felt *awesome* having it with me again.

"Are we feeling better now?" Lach teased. "Can we finally move this party inside? Where there's air conditioning, I hope?"

I rolled my eyes. It was barely spring, and only the faintest hint of the sea lingered in the air. Regardless, I allowed him to shepherd us toward the building I assumed Pyra had pointed out earlier. Ryder drew up beside me, the backs of his fingers knocking against mine at my side, and I offered him a smile, lips closed. "I'm good," I said, meaning it now.

He traced the outer edge of my index finger, eyes swirling with approval. "I know."

Pyra groaned as she dragged open the heavy steel door to the legal center—as the plaque on the wall beside the doors proclaimed. Lachlan jumped in for the assist, grinding his heels into the pavement dramatically as he wrenched the door back. He wiped some imaginary sweat from his brow as he propped it open. Pyra seemed to notice him for the first time, her eyes sweeping the length of the seven-foot-something elf.

He grinned maddeningly. "I'm not very good at saluting." He gestured us inside with a flourish of his arm. "But I excel at opening doors."

"And leaning on them, apparently," Ryder murmured in my ear. I stifled a chuckle.

Pyra's body heaved with a gusty sigh. Rather than follow me, she stepped closer to Lach. The top of her head drew nearly level with his chest. "I don't know you, but you were gaining some cool points because Zara habitually allows you within a twenty-foot radius of her person." She snapped and flames leaped to life in her palm. Pyra cradled them in the six-inch space between their bodies. "But you had to go and annoy me, so you just lost those points." Spirals of smoke curled upward as the fire went out. "Consider yourself in the red."

Lach's wide grin spread. "What's that mean?"

"It's not a place anyone wants to be." Her chin jutted out. "It'll take a miracle for you to climb out of that pit." She presented him with her back, spine locked, but when she walked by me, I swore she winked. "Hurry up. I may be a fan of not arriving on time, but we're well past the timeframe I'm comfortable being late."

Ryder brushed my neck as he meandered after Pyra, unwilling to match her sharp march down the shiny, waxed parquet floors. Lachlan's arm came around my neck, squeezing tightly as he dragged me after them.

"What's with you?" I asked. "It's like you've been running a million miles an hour... then we talked on the train and you were so twitchy and weird... but now you're back to your normal self again. Are you ok?"

"That was a low point for sure, but even smiles have valleys." He swayed merrily back and forth. "I swear, boss, the best day of my life was when you got the drop on me in the ring. Now it's all Dragons and centaurs shooting arrows at our backs and touring the elusive, exclusive Order Headquarters. Hardly ever a dull moment."

As he danced on ahead, I couldn't hold back my grin. He didn't make a lick of sense, yet I knew exactly what he meant.

Chapter 9

Directly across the hall loomed two closed doors. The War Room. My friends and I handed our bags to one of a half dozen soldiers in fatigues stationed outside. I didn't necessarily trust the guy who snagged my stuff, but it wasn't like I owned much of personal value to steal. I wore everything of importance on me.

"Alright." Pyra rolled fresh black tape around her thumb and middle fingers as if preparing for battle. "Did Joseph tell you how this is all going to go down?"

"Vaguely." I smoothed my hands down my shirt.

She nodded, but plowed ahead. "To refresh: in attendance today are us four Gods, three members of the new Council, and the two remaining High Priests—or whatever Seth refers to himself as these days." She cut the tape with her teeth and tucked the roll into her pocket. "Each person gets one vote, majority vote wins. Capisce?"

"Capisce."

Pyra wagged her thumb at Ryder and Lachlan. "They'll follow us in, but won't be allowed down on the main floor. Only a few others will be in the audience—mostly aides and trusted advisors. No reporters, though, the Order prefers to control its message." Her gaze focused sharply on Lach, who lifted his palms. I could have told her the warning wasn't necessary. The elf was more likely to burn the building down than share secrets with the press.

"Sit wherever you like, but don't speak," Pyra told the boys. "This discussion is for those gathered around the table and them alone. Think you can handle that?"

The boredom on Ryder's face didn't shift an iota, but Lach swooped his fingers across his lips, miming a zipper and lock. Pyra reached for the pocket where she'd tucked away her suckers, but stopped and squared her shoulders instead. She must have made a gesture that I missed because the captain lifted his hand and rapped on the door. The pinging echoed off the empty walls.

"Your fight with Sha will look like nothing compared to what's about to go down here," Pyra added, pulling me to her side. "Keep your Fire close, Zara, you're gonna need it."

The door opened from the inside and in we went. I barely noticed the soldier who closed the door with a soft thud at our backs and waited for my eyes to adjust to the complete darkness that rimmed what I could only describe as an arena. A hundred rows of padded theater seats ringed the main floor, divided equally by five long, downward-sloping ramps.

We started down one of those ramps and I was vaguely aware of Ryder and Lachlan branching off at our backs, but I kept my attention on the spotlights in the rafters that sent brilliant shafts of light down on a table at the center of the room. Markings on the table divided it into five sections.

Seth and Oron stood by the part of the table marked with a tri-peaked mountain, creepy bone masks firmly in place. Beside them, two men and a woman I vaguely recognized from television as the newly inducted members of the Order's Council stood behind an emblem of the organization: an O with a forward slash through it. To their left stood Joseph, alone, his arms crossed as he stared up at the dozen or so television screens that hung from poles ringing the arena.

63

The segment of table marked with my familiar cresting wave beside him was empty, and Pyra strode up to a man with long, white hair and a trim beard standing poised behind Fire's symbol. He greeted her with a stiff bow, his attire differing from hers only by the red ribbon trimming his collar and hems of his wide sleeves.

Aware of the focus on me, I took up my spot, hands clasped loosely behind my back. Glances were exchanged. Unease twined around my bones, bubbled in my blood. I knew most of these people, yet I felt... outside.

I didn't belong.

I nodded faintly at Oron, telling myself I was reading too much into it, and breathed out slowly through my nose. Their glances were perfectly innocent. I'd been gone for months. Maybe they were merely curious about how I'd changed.

I wondered where Ryder and Lachlan sat—and if Finn was here. The spotlights were too bright to see much beyond the four-foot concrete wall penning us in. I returned my focus to the table. "Good afternoon, everyone."

Judging by the slight pause before everyone responded with their affirmations and greetings, my opening line hadn't been what they'd expected. I imagined they'd thought I would apologize for my tardiness, but as far as I was concerned, I'd made it here as quickly as physically possible. I had nothing to apologize for.

Joseph was the last to recognize me, finally looking away from the screens, brow wrinkled as if he'd only now noticed my appearance.

"We wondered if you could take the time away from your busy schedule to join us," Seth drawled, voice clear behind his reptilian mask. "How fortunate we all are that you found it within yourself to leave the fan club behind and finally take your fated task seriously."

How someone like him now commands Davarius's seat is beyond my comprehension. Kaleal's soft words surprised me. She never spoke

64

about the other Gods, the ones from her era. *Cut him down to size, show him the weasel he is.*

Again, I didn't *want* to like Kaleal.

But then she had to go and say stuff like that...

And I was completely on board.

"Don't mistake my absence as disinterest." I leaned my weight on the table with the heels of my hands. "If you'd actually wanted my help, you could have reached me. Besides, it seemed you had everything in order... until you didn't."

His mask dipped, the eye sockets of his dragon skull leveling with mine. "Perhaps if you had been with your fellow Gods doing what you should have been doing all along—"

"I may be a God, but I'm also a teenager, one who didn't grow up under the umbrella of either the Order or any particular temple." I rolled my knuckles across the table. It wasn't plastic like I'd thought, but it wasn't wood either. "I left Oron and Pyra—who both grew up knowing what was expected of them—in charge of nuclear negotiations. And, Seth, I remember you saying before we left for Geneva you were more than happy to lend your expertise in the matter—that we *children* would need help fixing the world's problems."

I kept my eyes on those big, black sockets, wishing I could see his face. "Besides, High Priest Xi volunteered his efforts to assist Pyra." I motioned at the man with an expression so stony I doubted a sledgehammer could break it. "So, I fail to understand why you think *my* inexperience would have changed the outcome in the slightest."

The council members exchanged looks, mouths pursed, and Pyra gaped with open amazement. Five months ago, if anyone had asked me if I would publicly admit to and own my weaknesses, I would have laughed at them. But I wasn't that girl anymore. I'd grown enough, learned enough, during my time away to recognize I didn't have all the answers to everything.

Seth's silence radiated like poisonous smoke.

Well, now. Look at you. Kaleal slow clapped. *You've learned something from me, after all.*

"Now that we've cleared that up—" Magic flared, ripping the rest of the words from my mouth, stealing my breath.

"Enough." Joseph's coppery complexion had gone ruddy. He held his hand by his side, fingers straight as if he'd swiped through the air, silencing me. I rubbed at my throat. "We are here for one purpose, and that's to figure out how we're going to handle the debacle that is this global situation. We don't have time for childish posturing." Chilled fingers brushed up my spine as he speared me with a look. "Anyone have an issue with that?"

Quietly seething, I tore back control over my own oxygen. I didn't dare look at anyone else as they chorused their negative responses. Why did that feel directed at only me? Seth had started it. And why couldn't Joseph look me in the face without glaring?

"Cartwright, what's the latest?" Joseph directed his question at the bald man across the table, who nodded. He shoved his sausage-sized fingers into his suit pocket, drew out a silver-cased phone, and started reading from it.

The assessment wasn't great.

The hostile nations who'd pulled away from negotiations, crowing their superiority over the world, were offering sanctuary they couldn't guarantee to any nations who joined their cause. They already had seventy or eighty takers under their belt.

The other five nations with the most firepower had banded together with more than one-hundred other, smaller countries, and were discussing ways to spread their anti-warhead shields thinner than they already were. Not that it mattered. The shields were a sham. They could stop a warhead from making a direct hit, but it wasn't possible to isolate the air into one confined space, so the radiation from the blast would still fry everyone within minutes.

Because of that understanding, everyone was twitchy.

As militaries mobilized, most other countries ordered total lock-downs. Trade had halted. Economies were frozen. Civilians didn't dare go outside, pretending their homes would protect them from the fallout, preferring to air their fears and frustrations over the internet instead.

"What are our options?" I asked when Cartwright put his phone away. "Since everyone else is panicking about the eventuality of sucking down radiation rather than solving the heart of the issue, how do we move forward?"

"Simple. We take their weapons." Seth brought his fist down on the table with a bang. Beside him, Oron stood silently, hand braced on the scimitar at his hip. "There is no military bigger than ours on the planet. We move in, isolate the facilities, lock them down, and keep everyone out."

Seth's sandy-colored cloak billowed dramatically as he paced. "We've been training for a decade to override the controls. We merely need to access the launch codes. If the governmental heads don't want to hand those over willingly, we'll take them by force." His biceps bulged around the open sleeves of his vest as he leaned against the table. "If they can't access their weapons, they can't fire them. Problem solved."

The head of the Earth Temple motioned toward Joseph, who nodded in agreement, his long hair fanning around his face.

That threw me. He stood with Seth on that assessment? It felt overly aggressive to me.

"Why would those governments let us anywhere close to doing that? You think they'll happily turn over the controls to weapons of mass destruction? Just like that?" I demanded, heartbeat quickening. "Do you really think they're going to let us waltz our guys onto their bases and take over? I wouldn't."

"I'm with Zara," Pyra said. "We're only provoking conflict if we move in on our own. Fine, maybe some of the smaller nations will fold, but no chance the bigger ones will cave—military might or not. And even if we were to seize control, they'd launch a counter-attack. This is only going to end with death, violence, and destruction."

"Not unless we threaten the wrath of the Gods." The councilwoman spoke, holding up one elegant finger. A gold band encircled her dark skin. "There's a lot to be said when faced with the possibility of mass flooding or fires."

"Sonja's right," Joseph said. "Even something minor, like total darkness, would present a tremendous threat. We can force compliance if they won't offer it freely."

Pyra jumped all over that, lobbing arguments about how forcing compliance here wasn't any better than what was happening now. I barely heard her. My skin felt too tight, too hot. Buzzing filled my ears. Had I heard them correctly? No way had I heard what I thought I'd heard.

Kaleal's head shifted back and forth, following the volleying discussion while adding none of her normal input.

"You can't be serious." My voice rose above Pyra shouting at Sonja and Cartwright, who appeared to agree with Seth's idea. The lights overhead flickered. "Mass flooding? Total darkness? Do you hear yourselves?" I waited a beat, allowing the silence to sink in. "We can't throw that out there if we aren't willing to follow through. All it takes is one leader for us to call our bluff and that's it."

"Who says we're bluffing?" Seth's voice snaked through me, oily yet conflictingly icy. "Oron, if we threatened earthquakes and mudslides for non-compliance, would you follow through?"

The lanky boy lifted his hands. I had yet to hear him speak, since he preferred to use various sign languages, including my preferred brand learned from the pixies. I stared at him, willing him to hear me, *see* me, begging him to not agree with Seth.

But his fingers twisted in the affirmative.

I felt as if someone had slashed my guts and ripped my intestines out.

"I would, too," Joseph said quietly. "Tornadoes, darkness, whatever it took."

"No, you wouldn't." My voice shook. What was I missing between Seth and him? Joseph had hated Seth back in Egypt, but now they were perfectly aligned? "You don't know what you're saying."

I'd spent the last five months of my life saving people from these types of disasters, five months connecting with humans and fey alike, healing them of their wounds, learning their stories. To think my fellow Gods were now willing to threaten the lives of those very people with their own powers, their own *hands...*

"Come on, Zara, don't be naïve." Joseph's condescension tore another gaping hole in my side. I flinched. "The threat alone will be enough. Everyone's willing to face the potential of mass extinction together, but this—this is an individual threat. Either hand over your codes and revoke your access or your entire nation could be underwater. Not your neighbor, not the guy across town, only you."

"That's absurd," Pyra snapped. The surrounding air shimmered hotly. "Why wouldn't they launch the nuke in retaliation then? They've got nothing to lose."

Xi glanced at Sonja and dipped his chin. My fingers curled. Something wasn't right.

"Then what do you suggest, Fire God?" the third councilman asked. He fanned out his hand, a silent plea for peace. "What alternative do you offer?"

"We work toward diplomacy. Call everyone back to the table."

"And that worked so well the first time around," Joseph snapped.

"I wasn't finished." Pyra braced her hand on the table as if preparing

69

to hop on top of it, but Xi pinned her wrist down. He shook his head once. She hissed through her teeth, but drew back, standing to her full height instead. "So we failed back in Geneva. Maybe we weren't trying hard enough. Maybe we didn't present a unified front. Whatever the leaders of the other nations needed to see, clearly they weren't getting it."

She crossed her arms haughtily, eyes spitting sparks. "Maybe having Zara back, fresh from her campaign to improve public relations, will change a few minds. Or maybe, Joseph, maybe they needed to hear from you on the issue. You've skyrocketed in public opinion since you've turned the Order around so quickly. If the four of us stand together, we might prove that the rest of the world can stand together, unified, too."

I flipped my thumb at Pyra. "What she said."

But Joseph was already shaking his head, and that set Seth off again as he pounced all over her argument.

And around and around we went. No one offered any other alternatives, but also didn't appear to be swayed by the options on the table. The unsettled feeling that had gripped my gut the longer we argued spread. An undercurrent ran through the room, like a thread of magic I couldn't see.

The lights flickered, and the temperature dipped. Joseph held his hand high. "I say we vote on it. We're going around in circles. We have two clear paths, surely everyone can pick one by now."

Pyra caught my attention, eyes panicked, hands slashing down by her waist beneath the table.

A heavy weight settled against my lungs. I scanned the room. Seth, Joseph, Oron, and Sonja were highly vocal in their demand for action now, diplomacy later. I hadn't gotten a read yet on Xi, but even if he was on our side, I had a feeling at least one if not both of the councilmen were in favor of Seth's proposal.

We didn't have the votes.

The head of Davos elbowed Oron. His mask tilted my way a moment, then dipped as his hands came up. His sign language was clear, unhurried. "I second the motion to vote."

A shout sounded from near the top of the arena, near the door where Pyra and I had come through, but no one paid it any heed. Sonja drew her phone from her pocket and set it on the table.

"With two Gods in favor of the motion, we shall proceed with the vote. All in favor of taking immediate action and moving to seize nuclear weapons, vote aye. Those against say nay." Her voice was soft, like the patter of rainwater on the sidewalk. "In accordance with tradition, we shall start with the First and move clockwise around the table. Zara Ramone, God of Water, how do you vote?"

I scrubbed my palms against my thighs. From everything I'd seen and where I'd been, there was only one way I could vote. "Nay."

Sonja tapped on her phone. Something heavy banged in the hallway. More shouts followed. I frowned, squinting through the darkness. Should we check it out? The lights were too bright to see if the door had opened.

"Pyra Zhang, God of Fire, how do you vote?"

The girl barely reached my shoulder, but she owned every millimeter of her height. "Nay."

"High Priest Xi Qiang of the Fire Temple, how do you vote?"

The priest brought his hands forward, fingertips touching before his chest. His dark brown eyes flitted first to Pyra, then strangely—Joseph. My stomach soured. "Aye."

My ears roared. Pyra's mouth fell open. That was it. If I could have seen Seth's face, I probably would have smashed his grin with my fist. They had the votes they needed to bully the rest of the world into compliance. We couldn't possibly stop this now.

"You can't be—"

"Miss Zhang, please refrain from all commentary until the official vote is cast." Sonja flicked her stylus at the God, then back at her phone. "Moving on—"

A door crashed against the wall at the same time a deep voice shouted, "You can't go in there!"

Sounds of a scuffle, then a shriek, and a woman sprinted down the aisle, black hair flowing like a scarf behind her. Any of us could have stopped her, but the absurdity of the moment held us captive. Two soldiers chasing her attempted to grab the woman's arms as she jumped the short wall, but she pulled off some spinning ducking movement that sent one man crashing into the other.

"Stop that," she admonished, nudging one man with the toe of her daisy-printed Keds. "I've as much right t'be here as anyone. I'm Marinda Olsen, a priestess with the Water Temple." She faced us, palms flat against her chest, barely out of breath. "What've I missed?"

Chapter 10

What. Were. The. Odds.

The very woman I'd spent the past three weeks searching for had appeared out of nowhere.

I'd lost the ability to form words, staring at the witch's unruly hair and sunken, shadowed eyes that spoke of too many nights with too little sleep. The woman had squeezed her curvy figure into a long-sleeve shirt and dress pants that may have fit at one point, but settled awkwardly on her now, as if she'd thrown them on as an afterthought.

She shifted on her feet, one knee twitching slightly. "You *are* here, like the news said you'd be."

I couldn't place her accent, the way her tongue curled around her vowels and spit them out like hot coals. Her shoes squeaked as she approached the table. Ryder had appeared at the edge of the circle, arms folded across his chest, eyes narrowed with intrigue that matched my own.

Kaleal had gone silent.

"I follow the news, you know. Fascinatin' stuff you're up to, and when I heard you were havin' this get-together, I knew I had to break my one rule." She grabbed a chunk of her hair and tossed it over her shoulder. Xi gripped his chin, scowl deepening.

"Rule?" Pyra managed.

"Never leave my house. Much too dangerous. Between the poison-fingered knaves and the dragon-toothed nymphs, I dare not risk it."

I blinked. I'd met my share of nymphs, both forest and water. They stood about a foot high and weighed maybe a pound, dripping wet. 'Dragon-toothed' was the last adjective I would have used to describe the skittish, thieving creatures.

Marinda continued, oblivious to my inner musings. "But when I heard Zara was lookin' for me and then this all happened, t'was like a sign." She pressed her middle and forefinger to her forehead in reverence and bowed so deeply she nearly tipped over. I knew that sign. Others under my watch had made that sign. *I'd* made that sign. Was it meant for me?

Marinda snapped upright and marched over to me. Her long, uneven nails bit into my forearm as she passed, squeezing my arm in easy confidence. "You haven' voted yet, have you?"

Joseph sputtered and toyed with the rims of his glasses, sliding them up his nose only for them to slide back down again. I'd never seen the man anything short of composed, even in the heart of battle, and I couldn't decide which person was more fascinating to watch.

Something utterly bizarre, yet completely foreign, was playing out here.

"Not... yet," Sonja admitted.

"Oh, good." Marinda grunted as she hefted a copper-colored purse the size of a carry-on suitcase onto the table. As the council members backed away from the table, Pyra leaned over it, chin propped in her hands, black-tipped nails tapping a rapid tempo along her cheekbones. The witch wrenched open a zipper and dug into the folds of the bag, scattering ripped pieces of paper, chewed pencil stubs, and hairbands in her wake. "I have all sorts of ideas that'll help you get this all sorted out in no time."

Oron moved to my side, head canted. He snagged one of the stray pieces of paper and held it before his mask. His head tilted to the other side as he offered the diagram of overlapping triangles to me. The movement caught Marinda's attention, and she grinned hugely, lips peeling back to reveal a missing eyetooth. "Don't worry yourself with that. Jus' a rune I'm workin' on to cure lice."

The Earth God smoothed a hand over the black spandex obscuring the back of his head as if feeling creepy-crawlies making themselves at home. Pyra's ember eyes flared, a manic grin stretching across her face. I wasn't sure she'd so much as blinked since the woman had walked in.

The witch produced another piece of paper and flung it at Joseph, index finger extended. "Now, I'm thinkin' you can create little shields to wrap around the weapons when they are fired, and then detonate them in those bubbles. Then you, the Air one—" she flapped her arms uselessly— "use your powers to send them into space. Lickety-split, your worries are over."

Joseph turned the page over in his hands, index finger and thumb still fiddling with the end piece of his glasses. In a rare show of camaraderie, he flashed the document at me, revealing a piece of paper with two blank sides. He mouthed, "What is going on?"

I rubbed the bridge of my nose. This was the witch who'd saved me from the Order? This was the woman who'd secreted me away and ensured I had a family to protect me? Had it truly taken someone insane to save me?

Seth was squeezing his arms against his chest so hard I feared his biceps might burst. Xi tapped his chin again. A dawning sense of awareness filled his face.

Marinda bobbed sagely. "I know people, I do. Jus' last week I talked with Mr. Agard, smart man, he is. Thought we had a plan figured out, but then—" Marinda blew a raspberry. "Nope."

Agard. The president of the former U.N. Security Council. The guy who'd told me, under no uncertain terms, would he ever take my opinions seriously? She claimed Agard had given *her* a platform to speak? That didn't seem… probable.

Marinda started rattling off other names, other countries, other ideas, including something about the Gods putting an end to technology once and for all, but Xi brought her to a halt with a soft touch beneath her elbow. "Lucielle? Is that you?"

Joseph sucked in a gasp, his cheeks hollowing as he scanned the woman up and down.

Lucielle? Who was Lucielle?

Marinda—Lucielle—whoever she was—stilled. Her cheeks bloomed with blotchy red spots before she ducked her head. "The High Priestess died, Xi. She died in the bombings. You know that."

"No." Xi crouched down, peering up at her through her matted hair. "No, it is you. You escaped? Why haven't you said anything? Where have you been? Lucielle—"

"Stop calling me that name!" She grabbed her bag and pressed it against her chest, her grip forcing more notebooks and pens to spill from the opening. Joseph raised his hands. I shook my head, stilling him. I needed to hear this.

"I'm not her." Marinda's eyes spun wildly. "She died. Lucielle Johansen died in the temple with her baby. She sacrificed herself and her family to save that girl there." She pointed a pudgy finger at me. A small shockwave rippled through my chest at being addressed. Her accent dropped away as she grew increasingly frenzied. "Lucielle is long dead. There's no coming back from an execution like that."

Xi's slender brows bunched, and he glanced at Seth, whose mask twitched from side to side. "Alright, I understand. I must have been mistaken… Ms. Olsen."

She nodded slowly, then appeared to deflate, her entire body sagging as she accepted his words for whatever they were. Oron stepped up, hovering around the edge of the circle.

"I think we need to take a beat and consider our options. We should look at every idea presented to us before we decide," he signed. "I propose delaying the vote by twenty-four hours."

Joseph glanced at me, then at the woman who choked back audible sobs as she knelt on the ground. Finally, he nodded at Pyra. "I'm fine with that."

Sonja's voice was thready as she spoke from the edge of the ring, hood tugged low over her head. "Very well. In accordance with the rules of the Order, we shall meet again in twenty-four hours to vote on actions to take against nuclear warfare."

She and the other council members bowed and scurried up one long ramp. Seth and Oron followed in short order. Before departing, Joseph tipped his head once at the witch, then at me, a question and an order in the weightiness of his dark gaze.

I pursed my lips in silent acceptance. Marinda was my problem. I needed to stay with her. Well, me and Lachlan and Ryder needed to stay with her. She had come here for me. She'd helped me delay a critical vote—deliberately or inadvertently didn't matter. I needed to help her if I could.

When she passed by, Pyra rose on her toes, brought her lips close to my ear. "*Promedis ad,*" she whispered.

I closed my eyes, the familiar saying of the pixies both settling me as much as it stirred me up.

At your ready.

It was advice that had never steered me wrong before.

- - -

The spotlights dimmed and fluorescent overhead lights flicked on, sepia bulbs blinking and spitting as they warmed. In the front row, feet propped on the bars of the railing around the arena, sat Lachlan. He tore off a chunk of a granola bar in his lap and chewed. His other wrist rested on the curved top of TruthTeller's bow, strung and ready to go. I scanned the empty room, frowning.

"Ryder said to tell you he'll be back."

"That's enlightening," I drawled.

Lach buffed his nails on his shirt. "He wanted to get someone? Something about roses?"

"Roses?"

"I assumed it was part of your secret lovers' lingo. I tuned out about halfway through." He swiped a hand across his hat when I lifted a brow. "What? I'm not a messenger, least of all for him. The point here is: You need legal counsel more than a bouquet if I understand this nuclear vote right. Your incubus needs to get his priorities straight if he's going to woo you."

"Woo me?" I wanted to smack myself. I sounded like a parrot. "Never mind. Just sit there and look pretty. I've got work to do."

Contrary to what he'd told Pyra earlier, he flicked a lazy salute. "What I do best, boss."

A low chuckle and a clatter made me turn back to the center of the room.

"I used to wonder who you would surround yourself with when you came into your powers." Marinda rolled a blue tube of Chapstick between her fingers as she kneeled on the ground before shoving it into her beast of a bag. "They aren't the type you'd have grown up with had the Order not turned traitor, that's for sure."

Insult flared, the urge to protect those who stood beside me nearly swamping me. I tamped the heady emotion down, remembering to think before I acted. I dropped a bubble of silence around us, extending a small leg so Lachlan could listen. "You say that like it's a bad thing."

A harmonica joined the Chapstick. "Not in the least. It's refreshin', the changing of the guard."

That sounded like something the Thunderbird would have said.

"Thank you?"

The witch snorted.

I settled beside her on the ground and handed her some stray Post-It notes and foil-wrapped sticks of gum. "Are you ok? Things got intense there."

Curls flew as she shook her head. Another snort. "That's over and gone. How about you ask me what it is you actually want t'know?"

Alright then. Someone else who got straight to the point. Maybe that's where I got it from. "Why are you here?"

Marinda pushed a spiral notebook at me. Dozens of tiny white scars dotted her fingers. I paged through the book, smoothing the worn and wrinkled paper. She'd filled the pages with her handwriting, but it was so slanted and minuscule I couldn't make out a word of it.

"I didn't save you, only for you to fail when it counts. Besides, because I got you out, I have as much right to be here as anyone. I used to be in rooms like this all the time, makin' arguments like this all the time, I know what I'm doing… and I do have ideas."

The smooth, cool glass of Phenex's vial found its way into my palm. I traced its silver etchings, my thoughts blurring. Had Marinda admitted to being the Head Priestess? I could see her being a second and attending meetings, but if she voiced her opinions, wouldn't that make her one of the few leading the operation? Part of me didn't want to ask for fear of setting her off again.

"Was the library helpful?"

My fingers stilled, the silver rings strung beside the vial clinking lightly against the glass as they settled into place. "What?"

"The library. We left it in your care."

Kaleal ghosted forward, practically pressing against the backs of my eyes, index finger tracing the bow of her mouth.

"I'm sorry, but I'm not sure what you're talking about," I said.

The witch clicked her tongue and tossed her snarled hair over one shoulder again. "I told them it was a far-fetched idea. And I was right." She held out her hand and wiggled her fingers. "Haven' you unlocked your stabber yet?"

My hand dropped to my dagger. Her eyes tracked my movement.

"That's the one. We left you everything you needed to know inside of it—a fat load of good it did since you're more dense than we expected." Marinda wiggled her fingers again. "Give it here. And the rings, yes, I see them. I'll show you."

Yes, give the unhinged witch a sharp object to play with, Kaleal snarked, hands clasped at her chest. *I desperately need to see how this scenario plays out.*

You're as bad as Lachlan sometimes, you know that? I retorted. To the witch, I said, "Why don't you tell me what to do, instead?"

The witch shrugged and reached for a packet of cucumber seeds that had fallen near one of the table legs. "No matter to me, it's your stuff. But you need t'unwrap the base of your blade, first."

I tugged my dagger from my sheath, magic thrumming excitedly. Finally. Answers I'd craved for nearly a year were literally at my fingertips.

I felt along the leather wrapped tightly around the base of the blade with my fingernails until I found a slight groove. A twist and a tug, and it unraveled, exposing an extra length of blue-tinted metal. The leather, which I could now see had a rune etched into it, was the only thing preventing it from slicing my hand open.

Bearing that in mind, I used the wrapping to cradle the weapon in my hand, tracing the newly exposed steel. My nail caught on something engraved near the base, and when I brought it to my face, I realized... "It's the shape of the rings."

Marinda snorted. "Of course it is. One on each side. That unlocks it."

I removed my necklace and slipped the rings from the chain. I did as she instructed, fitting the head of each ring into the matching grooves on both sides of the flattened metal. The blade shimmered turquoise. I heard an audible click, and something black dropped into my lap.

I set the knife on the floor and held up the object. "A memory stick?"

"Not any memory stick." Marinda zipped up her bag loudly. "That there is the entire library of the Water Temple. Every book, every notation, every hypothesis, and forbidden conversation. All there t'help you on your way."

I blinked down at the plastic stick, no bigger than my thumb. Seriously?

Time and time again, the fey had told me the most extensive library in the world had been housed at the Water Temple. Everyone thought it had sunk into the sea with the rest of the Palace of Oceans... but they were wrong. I'd carried it with me all along.

My fingers shook, the realization of what that meant smacking into me like a bus.

This is too good. Kaleal dropped into a chaise lounge she called up with a flick of her smoky fingers. *You had all the answers you needed to solve that curse in the palm of your hand... and you never knew it. Oh, how I love irony.*

Never mind the dagger hadn't technically been in my possession these past few months. Never in my wildest dreams would I have thought to dismantle the weapon. Kaleal was right. I'd had everything I needed right here, and I'd never known.

Wait.

Everything I needed?

I glanced at Marinda, who'd settled back against one of the table legs, one arm pulling her knees tight against her chest. "Is there a book that can translate the original fey language?"

The language of *The Word*.

The book Joseph and I had tried again and again, unsuccessfully, to crack.

"Oh, yes. Tools to translate every language, actually." Her cheek pressed against her knee, purple bruises beneath her eyes deepening in the shadows.

My shoulders twitched, her uneven movements reminding me of a horror movie I'd watched as a kid, one where a little girl sat exactly like that when a monster possessed her soul before she scuttled backward across the floor.

"But I wouldn't worry too much about reading *The Word*, if I were you," Marinda said.

"How did you—"

"There's only one book of any real interest written in that dead language." Marinda coughed into her hand. "But it's terribly imprecise and riddled with plot holes an' misdirects. Not worth your time. It's why it's been rewritten so many times. *The Word* may tell the alleged story of the Original Gods and the origin of how modern magic was born, but the original text is too outlandish. We had to clarify the key points, or else the message would have been lost."

Kaleal, who'd been lounging comfortably, sat up straight, movements stiff as she crossed one leg over the other at the knee. I mentally replayed what Marinda had said, wondering what had signaled the God's attention.

I feigned disinterest as I tucked the memory stick back into the hole at the base of the dagger and began wrapping it back up, though I carefully monitored Kaleal's reactions, hoping she'd give something away. "Anything in particular?"

I sensed a disturbance in the air currents around our isolated bubble, but I didn't acknowledge it. Whoever it was would have to wait. It wasn't like they could hear us, anyway. Even Lachlan refused to be distracted. In my periphery, he'd bent forward in his chair, expression fierce, batting TruthTeller between his hands lightly as its end rested on the ground.

Marinda flopped on her back so I could only see her shins in her too-tight slacks. "Oh, too many to count, but there is this one line that ties everyone up in knots whenever a new crop of Head Priests and Priestesses get their grubby hands on the real deal. It's toward the end when the fey formed the Order and finally figured out how to strip the Originals of their power—you know, because they started all those wars for their own amusement, used their magic recklessly, all that."

Kaleal stood tall, face flushed, practically vibrating with intensity.

"So they've stripped Lyre, Davarius, and Ash of their powers. The two former ones went willingly—though, I've heard tales that Lyre was practically comatose by this point because of injuries inflicted during the war—but Ash was always a bit of a hellion, so he made them work for it." Marinda laughed brokenly, eyes focused on the steel beam rafters.

He was a fighter, Kaleal raged, surging forward. *The other two fell apart in the end, weak fools who glimpsed their true potential but never pushed hard enough to reach it. But not him. Not me. We knew what it was to reach for the stars... and when they were stolen from us... we wanted nothing but to get it back.*

She stormed around my mind, seething so hard I could practically feel the frustration wafting from her. I'd glimpsed many faces of Kaleal before: her cunning, her intrigue, her ire, her exasperation—her fear. But I couldn't recall seeing her so enraged before. It practically wafted from her in hot, heady waves.

"What people don't know is Kaleal was the real problem. Nowadays, everyone thinks Water is so docile because the newer Gods of the element tend t'stay in the background, but really, Kaleal was the driving force behind the darkness. A real piece of work, that woman." Marinda clicked her tongue.

Kaleal clenched her fists so tight I expected blood to drip from them.

She said something that sounded like a curse in another language, and I felt a sharp tug in my chest. My shoulders locked as I buckled down, resisting her efforts to take control of my magic.

Enough, I snarled, shoving her away. For months she hadn't so much as lifted a finger in opposition, but now she was practically on a warpath over a few comments from a witch who didn't even know the God was listening. *I'm not letting you attack her, so back down.*

The tugging stopped, and with effort, Kaleal released her fists. She dropped into her chaise lounge again, docile as a kitten. *Fine,* she agreed, far too quickly. *I'll behave.*

A sickness settled in my stomach, a rotten feeling that never went away. Yes, Kaleal was definitely plotting something, and I doubted I would know what that something was until it was far too late. But I didn't know what other choices I had. She'd already proven I couldn't lock her away, and I didn't know how to destroy her. Yet.

Marinda's voice grew louder. "So they've got her up on the crucifix and they're drawing the runes of binding. Before the Order members join hands to split her power from her body and direct them into the Kraken, she throws her head back—and this is the best part."

A cruel, cruel smile split Kaleal's face. A smile that made me flinch away from her and the icy steel of promise etched in every line of her body.

Marinda scrambled to her feet, arms outstretched, neck tilted in imitation of the beaten God, and shouted, "'You think you've bested me, but enjoy your pitiful peace while it lasts. I promise you, when the True God rises above the rest, you all will cower and quake—for through their unparalleled powers will I make my return and your descendants will pay dearly for your mistake.'"

The witch paused. The words seemed to echo, relaying their own kind of horrible power.

The God in my head stood and sketched a mocking bow. She locked eyes with me, her knowing grin cutting through me, as if daring me to contradict Marinda's allegations. But there was no doubt in my mind that what Marinda had said... was exactly what had happened.

I held her gaze, and Kaleal's grin spread before she disappeared in a curl of blackness.

"And then the Order stripped her of her magic." Marinda sighed deeply, chin wobbling as the glaze vanished from her eyes. She jerked one of her shoulders up. "She died not long after that, along with the other Originals. They'd lived long lives already, too long for this world."

I scarcely breathed. I could picture it in my head. Kaleal tied up, throwing herself against the ropes around her wrists, screaming at the skies as her violet eyes glowed, threatening to bring retribution down on everyone's heads.

Based on Kaleal's reaction, I didn't doubt that what was written in *The Word* was an exact retelling of that day. The drama and intrigue fit the soul of the woman I'd come to know so well. What I did doubt was the validity of her claim.

I believed Kaleal wanted to create a legacy that would ensure the world never forgot her.

I also believed Kaleal wanted to spread discord and to frighten people into believing in her power, believing she was invincible in her own way. It was what she did best—and I would know after everything she had done to me.

Worst of all, it had worked.

She was still here. And apparently people still worried about her. On top of all that, I still didn't know how to handle her, and part of me worried I never would. The Order still feared of her. So much so, they'd changed *The Word* in an attempt to hold her back.

Kaleal truly was the cleverest person I knew.

I swallowed hard, trying to slow the pounding of my pulse, and swiped at my nose, scenting cinnamon.

Cinnamon.

I glanced around, remembering the displacement of the air. Ryder now lounged beside Lachlan, elbow propped on his thigh, chin in hand, watching us closely. At his side, my former pixie bodyguard, Rose, grinned madly, bouncing in her seat. That's what he'd meant about 'roses.'

Our reunion would have to wait a moment longer. The witch watched me carefully, a wary gleam in her eyes.

"Do you believe Kaleal spoke the truth?" I asked. "Do you think she somehow ensured this so-called 'True God' would rise someday and bring her back?"

Marinda slung the strap of her bag over her head and patted its bulk. "Like I said, every few hundred to a thousand years the temples debate that passage. Some think it's prophecy, but most call it poppycock." She shrugged. "I'm with them. Kaleal couldn't possibly have anticipated or planned for somethin' like that. It isn't how her magic worked—or how any magic works."

I didn't need to hear Marinda echoing my thoughts to validate my beliefs, but I breathed a little easier because of it—knowing someone else hadn't fallen for Kaleal's claims hook, line, and sinker. And as long as others didn't believe in the weight of her influence as much as she wanted them to, I felt I still had a chance.

Kaleal was still locked inside me. She did not appear to have another way out. And as long as it stayed that way, as long as I maintained that upper hand, nothing was going to change.

It didn't matter how much fear she sowed or what she might be plotting.

Because I was the stronger person.

And I would make sure she never came back.

Chapter 11

"**I** can't believe it's you." Rose plastered herself against me outside on the plaza, rubber band arms attempting to crush my ribs. "You brave, strong, stupid girl, you."

"It's good to see you, too," I gritted, hugging her back. Several people stared, mouths cupped behind their hands as they walked by. I blinked back the wetness prickling my eyes. I'd left everyone in such a lurch back in Geneva. The fact nearly everyone had welcomed me back like this... it sucker punched me somewhere deep. "And what kind of greeting is that, anyway?"

The pixie released me and wiped away the streaks of moisture running down her clover-tinted cheeks. "I meant every word of it. And for leaving us all without a word, you owe me at least four training sessions."

I rubbed my shoulder where she cuffed it, ducking my face to hide my grin. "I can't wait."

"Good." The pixie hooked her thumb in her belt of thorns that was actually her favored bullwhip. "Your butt better be in the gym before dawn or I'm sending Briar to bring you in—and let me assure you, that's definitely not something you want to have happen."

"Briar is here?" I scanned the plaza. Fey mingled with the humans cutting across the central plaza, but none bore the familiar jade skin and dragonfly wings of my second favorite of the warmongering pixies.

"Is Briar here?" Rose mocked my voice and prodded my cheek with one blackened nail. "Of course she's here. The whole squad is here. I told you they'll be training tomorrow." She scratched an itch on the shaved half of her head. "They've drawn up a schedule of who gets to beat on you first. Have fun."

"Looking forward to it." I squeezed my lips together but failed to pull off anything remotely serious.

Rose had taught me so much when I'd been starting out. When I wallowed in depression after defeating Toren and his army, she'd help pull me out of my funk, day by day, showing me how to pour my energy into physical training, learning to defend myself, learning to fight back. I wouldn't be half as skilled now if it weren't for her forcing me to master techniques I should have had years to learn. I couldn't wait to catch up with her over an exchange of punches and magical combat.

Ryder cleared his throat, reminding me we weren't alone. He kept a careful eye on Marinda, who sat on the marble lip of a water fountain feature, knitting needles and navy blue yarn in her lap. She'd given me a lot to think about, and the weight of my dagger against my thigh, of the information I'd hidden inside it once more.

"Are there any computers I can use on campus? Anything secure?" I asked Rose. I wished Pyra had stuck around. She might have a better idea. "There's something I need to check right now."

The pixie frowned in thought. "How secure are we talking here? I have a laptop to send in my reports and stuff, but I'm not sure how secure it is, exactly. It's on the Order wi-fi if that helps."

I shoved my hands in my pockets, scanning the plaza. No. That didn't sound safe enough. I didn't know how open those connections were, and I didn't want just anyone knowing about the information I had yet—not until I'd had a chance to sift through it on my own first.

Rose must have read the look on my face, because she pointed behind me. "You know who would know? The guy in charge of everything around here." Despite being nowhere near the height of the spire I'd fallen from, the building she pointed at now was easily the second-highest on campus—boasting about twenty stories of windows. "I think you were here when Joseph started moving into the top floor."

That actually was a pretty perfect solution. Joseph and I had worked together on cracking *The Word* months ago. It only made sense for him to be with me when we finally figured it out. Besides, talking to him now would give me a chance to see what was going on with him—away from the eyes and influence of our peers.

Something light and bright like dandelion fluff rose in my chest, something that felt a little like hope. I glanced back at Marinda, who was quietly chattering to herself in what sounded like Gaelic, needles clacking.

"Would you mind looking after her for a bit?" I asked the pixie. "Make sure she doesn't get into any trouble? I need to ask Joseph a few things, and I don't want to worry about how she's doing or what she's getting into."

The pixie scanned the witch, her brow arching. Then she shrugged. "Sure. This should be interesting. I want to ask her about how she got past our guards, anyway. It'll help me fill out my report later." She clapped me on the shoulder. "You go do your thing. I've got this."

As she ambled over, I heard her ask what Marinda was working on as she climbed up beside her, fingering some of the yarn.

I jerked my head at Ryder who grinned, falling into step beside me as I moved toward the building Rose has pointed out.

"Sure you want me tagging along?" he joked.

I knocked my shoulder into his arm. "Of course I do. Otherwise I would have stuck you on babysitting duty."

The incubus glanced over his shoulder and shook his head. "I'm fairly certain that woman needs a contingent of guards to keep her out of trouble." I felt his resolve shift, his body stiffen as he tugged me a little closer. His voice lowered. "Does this meeting with Joseph have anything to do with what that woman told you?"

It thrilled me how quickly he cut to the chase. Since I'd dropped the barrier dividing Marinda, Lach, and me from the rest of the world, part of me had been dying to tell Ryder everything about our conversation, hoping he might help me see the situation more clearly. He was good at stuff like that.

"Sort of." I lowered my voice and made a show of scratching my nose to hide my lips. "She told me how to read *The Word.* She had a lot to say, and I don't know her agenda exactly." I recalled her changing accents, her cadences. Something didn't add up, but I didn't have the luxury of time to delve deeper. Not with a vote happening tomorrow. "But I think looking at that text myself will clear a lot up."

Ryder held the door for me as we entered the tower. More people milled about inside, most wearing camouflage uniforms and flat-billed caps. The incubus stopped at the front desk and asked a receptionist with violently purple hair something. She put her hand over the receiver of the phone, replied with a nod, and returned to her call.

"He's here," Ryder said. "I'll go up with you."

We pushed past a few clusters of people, cognizant of their eyes on us, and Ryder hit the yellow button to summon one elevator along the back wall. We stood in contented silence until we boarded the elevator to the right when its doors opened. Ryder waved off a soldier who tried to get on with us at the last moment.

Halfway up, Ryder hit the red button to pause the elevator. "What else did she say?"

I dove right in, telling Ryder everything Marinda had said, sprinkling in details about Kaleal's reactions. When I finished, he shoveled his hand through his hair, eyes unfocused.

"There's a lot to unload there," he said when we finally arrived at the top floor. He'd released the machine when I'd come close to wrapping up. Joseph's office was at the far end of the hall, one of only two on this level. I recalled it used to be Geoffrey's office, a huge one that overlooked the plaza. "If it's ok with you, I'll think this over while you meet with Joseph."

"Sounds good."

We stopped outside the door and awkward tension sparked to life. I shifted from one foot to the other, wondering if this was how things were going to be between us now. Ryder's biceps bunched again and a muscle feathered in his jaw. But rather than reach for me like I half expected him to do, half *wanted* him to do, he stepped away with a curt nod.

"See you in a bit." He rapped the door with a knuckle and walked back down the hall as a voice inside called for me to enter. With one last look at the incubus, I opened the door.

Chapter 12

A desk piled high with meticulous stacks of paperwork and surrounded by three large bookcases of legal texts dominated the cozy room. Behind the desk sat a man with a sleek goatee wearing a stiff wool blazer. He didn't look up as he shuffled through some documents. With his fountain pen, he tapped a page at his elbow with the headline *Appointments*, then returned to scribbling in a notebook as he propped open another book with two fingers. "Name?"

I tucked an errant piece of silvery hair behind my ear. "Am I interrupting?"

"You will be if your name isn't on this list, and since Mr. Windrunner doesn't have any appointments scheduled for the rest of the day, you may draw your own assumptions." He flipped a page in his book with the back of his pen.

"I see." I choked down a laugh at the insult. "Would that change if I told you my name was Ramone?" The scratching of his pen stopped. "Zara Ramone. God of Water. First of Four and a bunch of other titles I can't keep track of anymore."

With each word, the man lifted his head incrementally. The rest of him had gone strangely still. I could only imagine his racing thoughts. Then his shoulders straightened, and he finally faced me straight-on, watery eyes narrowed.

I grinned. "Ring any bells?"

"Ms. Ramone, wonderful of you to stop by." He carefully laid his pen flat across his notebook. "And while I hope you're enjoying your stay here at Order Headquarters, unfortunately, that doesn't change you not having an appointment. I hope you'll understand when I say Mr. Windrunner is extremely busy at the moment."

I admired his gumption. I really did. "Yes, I understand—"

"Wonderful," he interrupted in a tone that sent my smile sliding right off my face. The tone of a man chastising a child. He dragged the *Appointments* page in front of him. "If you'd like to schedule a meeting with him, he has an opening on—"

"No, I won't be making any appointments." I leaned over the desk. "You didn't let me finish, because I was going to say that yes, I understand your boss is *busy,* but so am I. And it so happens that we're both tackling the same problem." I flicked a finger at the page, causing it to rustle around the point of his pen. The man sat up a little straighter. "So, you'll need to understand when I say this is urgent, I mean it."

The man stood, eyes flashing briefly toward the door to my left, behind which Joseph's office lay. "Ma'am, this is highly irregular—"

"Yes." I shot out. "Yes, preventing the world from dissolving into nuclear ash is highly irregular." I pointed at the door. "I'm glad Joseph has such a dedicated guard dog, but I'll be letting myself in now."

I didn't wait to argue with him any longer and dipped around him to the door, relieved when I found it unlocked. The man protested again but didn't get any closer, and after darting inside, I shut the door at my back and leaned against it heavily, taking a moment to collect myself again.

After a beat, I recognized the eerie silence, the strange tension in the air, and looked up to find not one but seven people staring at me. I promptly forgot what I'd come in here to talk about in the first place. Joseph sat with his back to me and slowly swiveled in his high-backed chair. A look of tightly restrained frustration flickered across his face as he leaned across his U-shaped desk.

"Zara, now is not a great time," he said tightly. He'd changed into a black suit, one that made him look a few years older than he was. His long hair was tied back at the base of his neck with a strip of dark leather.

I eyed him, then the faces on the large screen at his back, trying to figure out why several of them looked familiar. "What's going on here?" I asked pleasantly.

His jaw flexed, dark eyes burning into me, though he kept his tone smooth. "I was in the middle of explaining to these reporters the latest developments in our efforts to end the nuclear standoff."

He was holding a news conference right now? That's where I recognized some of these people from. They were from some of the biggest international news stations. I'd only watched them in casual passing, so I didn't know them by name.

I approached the desk, and Joseph's face tightened incrementally with each step. His eyes flashed a warning, silently pleading with me to not do or say something stupid, and I felt a flicker of insult. Before I could open my mouth, Joseph made a snap decision and spun back around.

"Ladies, gentlemen, I apologize, but I'm afraid I have to cut this conversation short." He tapped a few keys on his keyboard. "I'll answer your questions sometime later today. My assistant will make sure you each get a release."

The screen went black as he ended the conference call. He also reached up, shutting off the webcam to be safe.

"So this is what Pyra meant by controlling the message?" I asked. My frustration mounted, though I couldn't explain why. "No reporters are allowed in the meeting, but you're more than happy to talk with them about it afterward? Without consulting any of the rest of us first?

What exactly were you telling them? We didn't reach a decision."

"And that's what I told them," Joseph said forced patience. He rose and faced me, arms crossed. "While our meeting may have been private, it wasn't secret. My phone hasn't stopped ringing with calls from leaders of nearly every country, demanding to know what our decision was." He motioned to the dozen or so flashing lights on the landline on the corner of his desk. "Everyone wants to know what we're going to do. They thought they were going to get an answer today. I'm the one who needed to tell them they'll have to wait another day to get their answers."

I shoved my hands in my pockets, feeling suddenly small. I hadn't considered he might have actually been busy when I'd barged in here. I hadn't known he was the one who talked to the media, that Joseph wouldn't have passed that responsibility off to some public relations peon.

"I'm sorry," I said. "I didn't know."

He thumped back into his chair, shaking his head with what I could only describe as sardonic irritation. "No, of course you didn't. And that's the problem."

My shoulders snapped back. A static charge buzzed in the room, lifting the fine hairs on the back of my neck. "What's that supposed to mean?"

Joseph ran his tongue across his teeth, gathering his thoughts. He held up a finger and turned to the three massive windows with warped glass propped open behind the desk. One of them hung open, and I heard the soft murmurs of people crossing the plaza below. While I waited for him to answer, I spun a slow circle, taking in the rest of his office.

The last time I'd been here, we'd raided the place, ripping open file cabinets and tearing through folders, searching for all the information we could about Geoffrey, his plans, and everything else he'd done as head of the Order. Now, all evidence of that brash day was gone, tucked away in bookcases and file cabinets that used to show their oak grains. Someone had since painted them white.

"Zara." Joseph said my name like a statement. A fact. "Sit. Please."

A chair before the desk shoved backward on its own. Despite the trepidation tapping a steady beat along my spine, I took a seat, my nails digging into the wooden arms.

"You have no idea what you've missed out on." He leaned forward, hands drawing together in a manner that reminded me eerily of Geoffrey. "You left everyone shouldering massive responsibilities, deliberately choosing to stay on the sidelines, and now, suddenly, you want back in."

My hackles rose, but I locked my physical reaction down, keeping my temper in check. I needed to hear him out.

Joseph continued matter-of-factly, "We are all keenly aware of what you've been up to these past few months, yet you know nothing of the trials and tribulations the rest of us have endured in the name of re-establishing peace and order."

Lava-like fury washed through me, bubbling up from my gut and spilling into my arteries, choking my lungs. It took everything inside me to not lash out, to snap something condescending. I hated how calm he was being about this, how casually he cut me down. How little he seemed to think of me.

"How about you spit out what you're trying so hard to not say?" I snarled. "The cameras aren't on right now."

"Fine. If you want my honesty, here it is." Joseph shot to his feet, face blank, chest heaving. "You've attended no meetings; you've relayed zero input. You didn't deal with the PR nightmare of resolving Geoffrey's actions, of pinpointing all the traitors, of drawing up their sentences.

"You didn't deal with the negotiations of nearly every nation in the world—getting them to trust in us again. You didn't help vote on the new council members, or draw up the paperwork maintaining our military presence, or unwind the unnecessarily complicated financial system left by the previous administration."

Sparks flashed, the static releasing its charge. I didn't feel any of it; I was too caught up in the lightning storm that was his eyes.

He reached for a remote beside the desk blotter and pointed it at the wall. A screen flickered on, one larger than the monitor on his desk. It was split into four rectangular boxes—one from Russia, another from the United States, even one outside our very gates. News outlets relayed footage of riots and demonstrations, people demanding peace clashing with others proclaiming war.

Joseph thrust the remote at the images. "I doubt you could tell me what the leaders of each of those nations is worried about, what each of them wants in order to maintain peace, under which circumstances any of them would be willing to give up their nuclear warheads, or why it's so damn difficult to get any of them to so much as look let alone speak with one another.

"Yet you come sweeping in here like you own the place and have the audacity to demand we start up negotiations again. That we look for every possible diplomatic solution like that isn't what we've been trying to do for the past few months." He slammed his hands down on the desk. "Like it's so simple and so easy. And best of all, you expect the rest of us to fall in line at your feet like you always do—despite having endured none of the same problems the rest of us have. You don't realize we are at our breaking point. We have done everything we can. And now we're here."

Flames I'd repressed for weeks scorched my lungs and I joined him on my feet, moving sinuously, like I'd observed Kaleal do time and time again.

"You're wrong, Joseph." I leaned across his desk, faces level, our noses practically touching. "I've played my role. I didn't understand anything that we were facing inside these four walls, or at the United Nations, but I've done more to establish trust and faith in our system than you'll ever understand. Without me on the front lines, meeting people, helping them out, we wouldn't be—"

"Oh, grow up already." Books crashed to the ground as a sudden wind howled. "You pissed away a bunch of time and energy getting your ego stroked while Oron, Pyra, and I worked our asses off." He slashed violently with his arm and a letter opener flew across the room, ending up embedded to the hilt in the wall. "You aren't seeing the bigger picture here, Zara. The *world* is at stake."

"People are at stake." I flung my chair across the room and rounded the desk. Outside, darkened clouds tumbled across the sky, obscuring the sun. Purple lightning flickered, followed by a boom that rattled the panes of glass. "*Lives* are at stake. Those on both sides of this mess. Human, fey, and everything in-between. You look at this and see a neat column of words and numbers." I snatched up an errant spreadsheet and held it out as another thunderous boom shook the room. Static electricity sparked. The power cut out. "But you aren't seeing their faces. You want me to be the one to destroy lives, to ruin livelihoods—to break entire nations. You want me to be a weapon."

I crumpled the page and threw it aside. "I didn't spend the past five months building this world back up only for you to tear it down."

"I'm trying to save them." Joseph's raised fingers curled into claws as if he longed to shake me, but he didn't. "I can't save them if nuclear bombs go off. We're *all* done if that happens. Done." Rain lashed against the glass, spraying us with mist through the open window. "Are you hearing me?"

I whipped around, slamming my hands down on the desk because if I hadn't, I would have punched him in the face, right between those lightning-storm eyes. I sucked air into my lungs, trying and failing to see past the dark haziness of my vision.

Too angry. I needed to calm down.

The side of my hand knocked into a sheaf of papers, exposing a corner of a book. Not any book. My vision sharpened.

The Word.

My copy. The one Finn had given me. I suddenly remembered why I'd come up here in the first place before the sight of all those reporters had derailed me.

Beneath the book was a page with scribbled writing. Chest heaving, I nudged the book aside, exposing the writing. A whooshing sound filled my ears when I read the words beneath my hands. They told a story. A story I'd just learned myself. Underneath it, someone had crossed out and circled two words again and again in thick, black ink.

True.

False.

When had Joseph cracked the language? Why hadn't he told me?

Marinda had said something about the new Priests and Priestesses arguing over Kaleal's claim every time they got their hands on the original copies of the text. In that case...

"When you say you, Pyra, and Oron worked in the trenches to deal with all the problems we faced, do you count Seth and Xi among the people helping you?"

"What?" Joseph sounded confused. "Yes. Of course. They've been indispensable." The static charge flickered, faded.

I shoved the book back over the story and paced away from the desk, face buried in my hand as I sorted through my racing thoughts. "They've helped you put the Order back together?"

"Yes?"

"And you've discussed this nuclear situation with them? Your strategies?"

"Yes."

I watched him closely. "Were they able to help you decode *The Word?*"

"Yes." He flinched, realizing what he'd inadvertently revealed, then steeled himself. "I read through it months ago. What are you getting at, Zara?"

"You and me, we both wanted to read what it said. But I haven't had the chance to, yet, like apparently everyone else." My voice had gone dangerously quiet, the moment between a rattlesnake's rattle and its strike. I remembered what Pyra had said at the gate, about Seth and Joseph trying to hold a vote before I arrived, trying to edge me out. How they were upset with me for being late, even though I rushed as quickly as I could. "Does it say anything I need to know?"

At Joseph's back, the skies were blue again. Tranquil. Such a contrast to the turbulence stark on his face. He opened his mouth, eyes seeking out the book, then closed it again. He swallowed hard. "No. It says nothing of consequence. It's all stories."

I nodded, my teeth clenching, hinges of my jaw pulsing. "Then why won't you meet my eyes?"

Now his eyes snapped to mine. "What is it you want me to say?"

My stomach knotted so badly I didn't think I'd ever be able to unravel it. Between the realization that Joseph was harboring such negativity toward me... and knowing that people in my inner circle were keeping secrets from me, for reasons I didn't understand, my entire being had cracked open.

"What are you hiding from me?" I ground out.

His eyes skittered away from mine again, a flicker to the left I wouldn't have noticed if I weren't watching so pointedly. "I'm not hiding anything you wouldn't have known if you'd been here, beside us, these past few months."

I was so mad I was shaking. "Care to fill me in now?"

"No. Because it's not important now. It doesn't matter."

"I see. So that's how it's going to be." Before I said or did anything more I might regret, I turned my back on him and threw open his door, striding out while battling back twin urges to cry and set the world on fire.

Chapter 13

I skirted a puddle and tugged my collar higher on my neck, wishing Lachlan hadn't vanished so I could steal his hat and cover my hair. I'd gotten used to people staring in general, but the attention was tenfold here, and I'd hit my limit. Hard. I needed to escape. I wasn't sure where I was going, only that I needed to get there *now*.

Every step was punctuated with a thought about my relationship with Joseph. I'd known we'd drifted in my absence, but I hadn't expected our relationship to have deteriorated like this. I'd always thought we were friends, that our viewpoints aligned, but the man in that room... he hated me. And if he didn't hate me, he was very close to it.

I wondered about the signs I'd missed, the clues I'd overlooked regarding our degrading relationship. He had been terse during his visit to Las Vegas, but I'd attributed that to the stress of the situation. Thinking back now, that should have been my first clue.

He'd barely wanted to be around me.

My foot landed square in the middle of another puddle, and I cursed, shaking the droplets from my boots. The contact with my element must have been enough to send my emotions shooting to the Kraken because Its tentacled form entered my thoughts.

Zara, I can help you if you'd let me in. It was the closest my Great Beast had come to begging. *I feel your pain, your frustration. I want to help. Together we can find a way forward...*

Not until you're ready to talk to me first. I was so sick of people not being upfront with me. Sick of not understanding motives or where I stood with them. My fingers clenched in my pockets. *If you're not ready for that, then get out.*

I longed for the days when I hadn't shared my mind with two other beings, worrying about them constantly listening in. I missed the days when swimming was my only concern. Everything had been so much simpler back then.

A hand grabbed my shoulder, and I snapped around, ribbons of water rising around me, ready to attack the person who dared— "Finn."

The silver studs in his eyebrows and nose twinkled in the midafternoon sun as he scanned first my face, then the serpents of water, and finally my clenched fists. This was so not how I'd envisioned seeing my guardian for the first time since we'd parted ways back in Vegas.

The kelpie didn't relinquish his grip and tugged me closer. "I've been yelling your name for a few minutes, but you didn't respond. What's going on? Are you ok?"

I wanted to burrow into him, to allow him to comfort me like he had so many times before. Finn and I may have had our differences in the past, but he would always and forever be my guardian, my protector, the kelpie who taught me to embrace the wonder that was my magic. But—

"Did you know?"

The wind ruffled his punk-shaggy hair and his bangs fell over his brilliant green eyes. His normally open expression revealed nothing. "Come on." His long fingers wrapped around my elbow, his grip strong as he led me away from the sidewalk to a bench partially obscured beneath the viny branches of a willow tree, granting us a small measure of privacy.

He sat on the seat first, the weather-beaten stone pale against the dark gray of his skinny jeans, then tugged me down beside him. It wasn't comfortable. I liked that.

"What are you going on about?" He angled himself so his back was against the arm of the bench, and pulled his legs up beneath him. "You're upset. What happened?"

"Did you know Joseph hates me?"

Finn traced his collarbone.

"Did you know he resents me? That he wants nothing to do with me?"

My guardian's head tilted, his chin dipping closer to his chest. But it was all in his face, he knew. He definitely knew. I scooted backward so my back, too, pressed against the opposite arm of the bench, mirroring his posture.

"You knew. You've known this whole time."

"Z, don't do this."

"Why didn't you tell me?" The volume of my voice rose, but I couldn't help it. I'd thought everything was good, that everything had been fine. But now the cracks in my universe were showing, and through them—I saw nothing. Only black, dismal nothingness. "When did this start? Did Seth influence him? Is he upset I left?" My voice cracked, and I hated myself for it. "What is it? What did I do?"

"You're putting me in a difficult position." Finn picked at the chipped blue polish on his fingernails, but the action didn't disguise his shaking. "Joseph's my boyfriend, and you're my friend—my leader. Don't put me in the middle of you two. Please."

My nails ground into the slab beside my thighs, shredding the soft keratin. "The way I see it, you *are* between the two of us. Square between us." Finn winced, his eyes squeezing closed, but I plowed on, giving voice to the venom eating me alive. "How else am I supposed to see you, Finn? At least give me *something*."

Fire and ice clashed in my chest, bubbling lava icing over, then erupting in a molten geyser, only to smash against the icy mountain of my soul. Over and over again. It hurt. This, right here, *hurt*.

Finn covered his mouth with his hand, a pained whine escaping his throat. Part of me felt guilty, attacking him like this, forcing him to decide on an answer, but another part of me, the part of me that urged me to keep pushing forward, to keep overcoming every obstacle in my path—that part of me demanded absolution for this betrayal.

"Joseph, he..." Finn opened and closed his hands on his thighs a few times, his body curled in on itself. "He grew up in that camp, Z. He grew up alone, waiting for his life to start. He dreamed of adventure, of going places. And... he finally got an opportunity to do that when you showed up and we whisked him away." He paused, stared up into the leafy canopy sloping over our heads. "But then you vanished."

I could barely breathe. I didn't want the sound of air moving through my nose to cover a single word.

"And you shackled him to a job that, yes, he's more than capable of handling, but you cut him off at the knees." Finn kneaded the back of his neck, knee bouncing out of control as he jiggled his foot on the grass. "Zara, Joseph is angry. He's so angry, and it's eating him alive. Yes, he does... resent you right now. And that's his jealousy talking. I don't think he'll always hate you, but he needs time."

Jealously.

Joseph was jealous of me.

And he hated me.

Right there in stark black and white.

I braced my elbows on my knees and dropped my head into my hands, sinking into the small amount of darkness they offered. I'd done this. I'd kicked the foundation of our trust. I'd initiated that first crack, and now... now here we were. Barely allies.

I'd done this.

"I've said too much. Please don't ask anything more from me about this," Finn pleaded thinly. "He's already going to be livid I told you this much."

I lifted my head, meeting his tortured gaze. I saw how much this was killing him, standing between us, being pushed one way and pulled another. I shoved back the ugliness clawing up my throat, swallowed it down, shoved it deep inside me where it didn't hurt so much.

"I understand," I murmured.

"No, don't do that." Finn grabbed my arms and dragged me to him. I didn't protest. "Don't shut down like that. You need to solve this. You guys already started figuring things out if that storm earlier meant what I think it meant."

"I don't think I can, Finn." I didn't push away, but I didn't relax, either. "I don't know how to begin. There's so much wrong here, and... I don't know."

The kelpie shook his head. "You *can* do this. I know you can. You both have such forceful personalities, and you're both so much alike—more than you know. All it would take is one of you copping to how you feel, and I guarantee—"

"I need to process this," I said slowly, meaning every word. "I don't know how to feel right now." That was a lie. I felt flayed open, my ribs exposed, both in terrible agony, yet disturbingly numb all at once.

"Yes, you do." Finn released me. "I know you do, and you need to face that. It's ok to feel what you're feeling, Z. Even if it's painful and ugly and selfish." I swiped at my cheeks, surprised to find them moist. I hadn't realized I was crying.

Finn linked his fingers together. "I understand why you left. I know what you needed to do for yourself. I know it and he knows it. We all know it. But sometimes doing what's right for you isn't what's right for someone else." He bumped my shoulder with his knuckles. "This can be fixed like anything else. But both of you have to try."

The tenderness in his expression, the honesty shining through his eyes, I couldn't handle it.

106

"It's too much, Finn." A bubble of lava burst, lancing my insides with molten heat and flaming rock. I knocked him off the bench with a slash of wind. I knew this wasn't how I should be handling this, yet incapable of doing anything about it. "I need to think. I need you to leave me alone."

"Z—"

I sent up a wall of water, forcing it to swirl around me, faster and faster, driving him back as I pushed him away until I was obscured behind a curtain of leaves and branches and swirling winds and lashing rain, taking care to keep the storm tight around me. I couldn't see Finn anymore, couldn't hear him. I didn't know where to go, didn't know who to talk to, and I was about to explode.

I didn't know how long I sat there, curled in a ball on the bench, the slab digging into my hipbone as my eye of the hurricane swirled around me, blocking me from everyone and everything. I didn't know how many tears I chased off my face, how many screams ripped from my throat, how many times I tapped my oaths in a poor attempt to regain control.

I didn't remember laying down, resting my head on the pillow of my arm.

But I did remember the hazy dream that followed. I remembered the soft curse and the arms that bundled me up, lifting me against a chiseled chest that smelled of fire and spice, of *home*. The jostle of my body as the incubus pulled me tight against him, as if I weighed nothing at all.

"You've outdone yourself this time, glowstick."

I remembered a pair of lips pressed a soft kiss to my forehead, and I hummed low in my throat, appreciating his comfort. I burrowed into Ryder's shirt, wondering why it was men's attire was so much softer than women's. "Let's get you back to our room."

Our room.

Implying we shared one.

I liked the sound of that a lot.

- - -

I jackknifed upright in bed, hand smashed against my chest to prevent my heart from slamming through my ribs. Ryder froze in the act of pulling his shirt over his head, tired amber eyes visible over the collar.

"You ok there?" he rumbled.

I tugged my knees up, getting a feel for my surroundings. Sheets beneath me. A bedside table to my left, a chest of drawers to the right. A bay window with a pillowy cushion that reminded me of a cloud. Another door that opened to what was surely a bathroom.

"It wasn't a dream."

The incubus chuckled and tugged his shirt back down, covering the twin divots near his waistline. "If you're talking about starting the mini hurricane that freaked the starlight out of Finn, subsequently burning yourself out, and me carrying you back here, then no, that wasn't a dream."

I buried my face in my hands, the tips of my fingers digging into the unraveling loops of my braid. "Oh Gods."

"To be fair, you've had a bit of a day." The bed dipped when he sat down. His hand found my calf, and he stroked the muscle, pulling it into his lap. "May I confess something?"

I lifted my head. The moonlight filtering through the window cast sinfully deep shadows across his face. His eyes turned to liquid gold. "What is it?" I asked warily.

"Lachlan and I bet on when you'd lose it."

I was getting too predictable. "Who won?"

"That elf of yours has less faith in you than I ever will, so, he won."

"Naturally."

Ryder pulled on my other leg. I resisted playfully, but he held on until I relinquished control, allowing him to tug it into his lap. We must have gotten back to the room a few minutes ago, because I still wore my jacket and jeans. I wondered if he would have removed them to help me get more comfortable. Heat flooded my cheeks, and I cleared my throat, thankful for the dark.

"Do you want to talk about it?"

I knew Ryder wasn't asking about my sudden shyness. "I—can we not talk about Joseph? In detail? I'm not ready to go there, yet."

"That's fine." The incubus rolled my jeans so they bunched at my knees. The callouses of his fingers felt wonderful against my smooth skin. I pulled off my jacket, longing for a little more freedom of movement. "What are you thinking about, then? What Marinda told you?"

Marinda.

I'd forgotten all about her. I shot upright, ready to bolt out the door, but Ryder held fast. "She's fine." His fingers dug into the bottom of my foot, and I nearly groaned. "Rose got one of her pixies to look over her. You need to stay here, relax, and recharge before tomorrow's vote. Now talk to me. No secrets, remember?"

I sagged against the pillows, gazing up at the ceiling, searching for shapes in the textured pattern. "I don't understand why no one told me about that story before, since it sounds like it's historically drawn a lot of drama. Them not telling me..." I tugged on my lower lip. "It makes me think they believe it's a prophecy, that they think this 'True God' will rise one day, and that Kaleal will be back. I can't help but wonder if they think I'm that person, given what I can do."

My hands opened and closed uselessly, the magic humming beneath my skin.

Ryder drew a breath. "Do *you* think the story's true?"

I turned Ryder's question over in my mind. "No. I don't. I've learned a lot about magic these past few months, and there's absolutely no way, from what I know, that Kaleal could have predicted something like that. There's no way, with her magic, that she could have set something like that into motion. She wanted to scare people. That's what she does."

Ryder's hand stilled. "She scares you?"

I liked this, the ease of his questions. Not accusatory, not demanding. They were merely questions. Straightforward and simple.

"Sometimes," I admitted. I wondered where Kaleal was now; wondered if she had come forth when I sank into my hurricane of emotions. I couldn't feel her roving my conscious thought like I normally did. "She's extremely powerful and very manipulative. She's tried to hurt me on any number of occasions—yet she still tries to save me. It doesn't make sense, and I think that's what I fear the most. I don't understand her and I don't know what she wants or when she'll push to achieve it."

Ryder rolled my jeans down and lifted my legs out of his lap. I didn't let him go far, snagging his sleeve until he dropped beside me. I wrapped myself around him, our arms intertwined around one another, scrunched against the pillows. I dragged my nails through his hair, massaging his scalp. He hummed and traced the oaths he found on my arms.

"Is there more?" he asked.

I gnawed my lip. Released it. "I don't like the phrase *True God*. I can see maybe they look at me and the three elements I control, and think, 'that's never happened before.' But no one could possibly know what it means. What if my magic has nothing to do with anything? What if Kaleal meant someone true to her name, to her memory, to her violence, to her cause? Not 'true' in the form of having more abilities. That's not me. I could never be that person."

I rested a hand on Ryder's chest. He closed his eyes and threaded his fingers through mine, his palm flat against the back of my hand. Right now, in this moment, things didn't feel confused between us. I didn't feel my usual urge to tug away, to create distance. I just let myself... be.

Maybe I needed to do this more often.

"I wonder if Pyra and Oron are in on the secret. I bet they knew about the 'True God' thing." I recalled the shifty glances, the unspoken words, and felt confident in my assessment. They clearly hadn't wanted me to know something. "How do I confront them about this? Do I need to?"

Ryder touched his forehead to mine, our noses brushing. "I won't tell you what you need to do, because you already know what you need to do." His hand moved up, covering the back of my head. "You have a strong moral compass, and you follow it without question. Let it guide you. Trust it to tell you when you lilt in the wrong direction."

The image of a compass formed in my mind and I held it close, liking how that sounded, the poetry of it. Lachlan had said it right before, Ryder did have a way with words. "And the vote?"

"Do I need to repeat what I said?" His tone was teasing, like the brush of his thumb along my jawline. I shook my head on the pillow, finally releasing a sleepy smile. "Didn't think so."

"Ryder?"

"Yes?"

"Will you stay with me? Like this? Tonight?"

"You don't have to ask."

Chapter 14

I recognized the soldiers manning the entrance to the War Room and smiled at them as they opened the heavy doors. I peered past the bigger one into the auditorium beyond, immediately noticing the lack of mood lighting.

"You've got about five minutes before the meeting starts," the skinnier one said with a pointed look at his digital watch.

"Who all is here?" I asked.

The bigger one grunted, handlebar mustache twitching. "Mr. Windrunner's been here about an hour, but aside from that, you're the first we've seen."

"Oh, perfect. Then I'm not the last one again." I rubbed the back of my neck and flicked them a small salute in thanks. They returned it with expressions of vague bemusement before I jogged down the aisle and took my space at the table. I deliberately didn't look at Joseph, not sure what to say to him.

I hadn't gone to see him this morning to either make amends like Finn had suggested or ask him again about what it was he didn't want to share with me. I hadn't gone to get my ass kicked with Rose. Instead, I'd left the warmth of Ryder's arms and sat in our bay window, legs curled beneath me, hand propped against the glass.

And I'd thought.

I'd thought about what Joseph had told me, about the resentment that festered between us. I also thought about what Marinda had revealed to me, and what more I needed to learn.

I had a plan, and I felt confident about it.

Casually, I scanned the surrounding seats. I wasn't sure how many people had watched yesterday, but this afternoon, only a few dozen seats had bodies in them. Most were absorbed in their laptops and cellphones, frantically typing away. Others, like Lachlan, perused the perimeter of the room, stopping to take in the symbols carved into the walls.

Ryder leaned back in his chair in the second row from the front, darkly handsome in his usual all-black attire, his legs propped on the back of the chair in front of him. To his right, hovering midway between my portion of the floor and Joseph's sat Finn. He twisted his fingers together, again and again, worrying the silk tie of a suit I'd never thought I'd see him wear.

A door opened and Xi entered, Pyra keeping languid pace behind him. He walked beside Marinda, and she laughed as he escorted her to her seat in the front row, directly behind me. She patted his hand, swung her hair from one side of her neck to the other, and waved him on.

She caught me watching and winked conspiratorially.

I didn't want to know what that was about.

"She's so weird." Candy clattered against the back of Pyra's teeth as she stopped beside me and offered a Jolly Rancher. Blue Raspberry. I declined. She shrugged, gaze fixed on Marinda as she piled a bundle of ivory yarn into her lap. "Spouting off insane statements one day, then cozying up to Xi the next. It makes zero sense."

"What makes everyone so sure she will not jump up here today?" I asked.

Pyra blew air out her nose. "Xi talked to her. He told her no matter what she did back in the day, she can't stand at the table and vote since

113

she isn't the High Priestess of the Water Temple." She snapped and casually flicked a tiny flame across the backs of her fingers. "She's sticking to that story, though everyone knows it's B.S. I've seen the portrait myself. No way she isn't Lucielle. But it's not worth the hassle arguing with her."

"Huh." I didn't know what to say to that.

The murmuring of the crowd picked up volume. Seth and Oron had entered from the right, Seth taking the helm as I expected, his barrel of a chest leading the way.

Pyra flicked the flame faster, not deigning to look at the last arrivals. "Marinda claims she accomplished what she came to do, which she said was 'expanding your vision and offering you illumination.' That's a quote by the way." She squinted up at me, red irises hot and bright. "So tell me, did she expand your horizons?"

My stress had sprouted spikes overnight, transforming into little balls of sea urchins in my belly that refused to go away. "Yeah, she did open my eyes to some things. Things I probably should have known a long time ago."

Pyra's stenciled brow lifted. The flame in her palm extinguished with a hiss, and she bobbed her head to the side, a hint of approval lining her lips. "That's good. I'm glad to hear it." And she moved back to her position at Xi's side. I assumed that meant she, too, was privy to whatever it was Joseph knew.

I remembered something Ridley had told me once: Face everything as a threat. I hadn't taken that advice seriously at the time, but the more the world around me unraveled, the greater my appreciation for his wisdom grew.

"Attention everyone." Sonja clapped her hands three times and the whispering and clattering of keyboard keys from those around us died away. Everyone at the table drew closer. "Today, on the twenty-first of April, we reconvene to confirm the action the newest coming of the

Gods will take in stopping the acts of nuclear aggression."

Fancy words for a not-so-fancy demise. I traced my thumbnail with my middle finger, keeping my expression vacant, my eyes downcast.

"I'll briefly recap our discussion from yesterday, and will open the floor for additional debate. After that, we shall proceed with the vote." Sonja scanned us, chin up, as if daring one of us to defy her instructions. Nope. That worked fine for me.

I forcibly relaxed my shoulders, mentally counting my oaths, and listened to the councilwoman describe the options presented to us. She tactfully skipped the interruption that was Marinda and outlined the votes already cast.

"Those votes are scratched, so those members may vote differently today should they so choose." Sonja's plump, purple-painted lips pursed. "I open the floor for debate. Ladies and gentlemen?"

"I don't see what's possibly changed in the past twenty-four hours." As I'd anticipated, Seth barely waited for the sound of her last syllable to fade before pouncing. "We went round and round yesterday, debating the same two ideas, with no one giving or taking. The world outside is waiting for an answer, and everyone's only growing more anxious. Putting off the vote was a waste of time—time we don't have."

Pyra jabbed a finger into the table. "When lives are at stake, there's always time to weigh the options carefully. Perhaps sleeping on such a detrimental issue gave some of us the *perspective* we need." She flicked her hair haughtily, arms crisscrossing her chest. "Or so I hope, anyway."

Seth wouldn't let that insult go unanswered and fired off a retort I barely heard. It felt strange, the lack of buzzing in my head. I'd thought this decision would feel more confused or frustrated, but for the first time in weeks, I felt strikingly awake, aware.

When Pyra moved to jump on the table and get up in Seth's face, I finally spoke, my voice pitched as if I were talking to someone at the dinner table: soft, controlled, concise. "What about the True God?"

I may as well have shouted because the effect those words had was instantaneous. Joseph's head swiveled, his jaw hardening. Pyra pinwheeled away from the table, a catlike grin spreading across her cheeks as Xi's eyes narrowed. Seth fell quieter than Oron, and the council members didn't dare make eye contact.

Yes, they knew. They all knew. Including Pyra, the one God here who still seemed to consistently have my back. The only one who, for all I knew, wanted me here at all. I swallowed back my hurt and allowed the silence to build, wondering what they might say.

"How do you know about that?" Joseph's words were an icepick to the perfectly frozen surface of everyone's fixed attention.

I resisted the urge to grip Phenex's vial as I stared down my friend or whatever he was to me these days. "Someone told me the *story* yesterday." I stressed the word 'story' with exaggerated calmness. "But what's interesting to me is none of you seem especially confused or surprised to hear that combination of words put together. Which makes me wonder... how long did all of *you* know? And why didn't you tell me?"

"It's not relevant." Joseph stepped closer, his toes brushing the engraved line separating my space from his. The world around me narrowed. "Like you said, it's a story, a make-believe tale borne from the mouth of a woman frustrated with having finally met her match."

"So what, exactly, was the harm in telling me a story?" I demanded. "If it has no bearing on anything?"

Joseph shivered as the temperature dropped, our breath puffing from our mouths in small clouds. He could have countered my magic, but he chose not to. It surprised me, the ugliness twisting inside me, the mutual understanding that of the two of us, I was the more powerful.

His eyes darkened, flicking back and forth between mine, begging with me to understand something I had no desire to decipher.

A sharp rap on the table snapped our little world, and the darkness clouding my periphery receded. It was Oron who lifted his hands, signs forming on his fingers in quick explanation.

"Kaleal lives within you." That sentence rang a chord inside me, a long, thin one that sent trills down my spine. "We worried she might not remember what she said, and if she were to remember the words she spoke that day, she would use them to manipulate you."

"He's right."

I closed my eyes, then turned to Pyra. She shrugged apologetically. "I didn't want to hide it from you," she continued, "but we decided it seemed strange that you had control over three elements. That hasn't happened before. We thought those might be qualities a… True God would have."

She shifted her weight. "Also, I know how awful Kaleal can be, how she can influence you sometimes, and I wanted to protect you. It seemed, at the time, the best way to proceed was to hide that particular story from you."

That took me aback. Her concern was touching and sounded reasonable.

But then Kaleal slunk forward from her corner of the oily shadows in my mind. *Isn't this rich,* she said. *They've got your number, don't they?*

Shut. Up, I snarled through clenched teeth, feelings of goodwill evaporating. She may have manipulated me in the past, but not anymore. Not for weeks. I'd finally ripped her from her mighty pedestal, proving to her who was, in fact, the more powerful between us.

Kaleal had no place here.

Pressure built in my temples. "How, exactly, did you think Kaleal would influence me? That she would convince me I was—what?—this fictitious *True God*? A title she made up as the Order severed her from her magic? You thought she would convince me it was my job to rule the world? Or better yet—to take over my body so *she* could rule the world?"

Ding, ding, Kaleal murmured, amethyst eyes alight with twisted humor.

The continued silence told me everything I needed to know.

Smoke curled from my fingertips, but I shoved down the urge to set something on fire. Deep down. "I appreciate the concern, but you have no idea what I've gone through to make sure that doesn't happen. You have no idea how much effort I've taken to *not* listen to the monster living inside my head."

Air hissed between my teeth and I forced myself to calm down, to slow the erratic thudding of my heart, and I went for honesty, hoping it might earn me some in return. "It hurts you assume I'm the one who is the problem here because I happen to control three elements. And that's how you justify shutting me out—and then acting surprised when I figure it out for myself." I flattened my hand against my sternum. "Tell me, in your readings of *The Word*, is there any mention of anyone having that kind of power before? Or any explanation for it *whatsoever*?"

"No." Xi's voice was satin-soft. "There is no explanation."

"So it might be connected to this stupid story Kaleal invented to scare people into submission, or it might be connected to absolutely nothing at all, right?"

The three council members glanced at one another and reluctantly nodded. Pyra didn't hold back and mimed firing a gun with her pointed fingers. "You betcha."

I couldn't get a read on Seth or Oron, though the tremble of Oron's hand on the hilt of his scimitar betrayed something. However, it was Joseph I was most interested in, the oldest of our group, the guy who'd taught me the fundamental principles behind magic, the God who'd laughed with me on the side of a pyramid and had fought beside me in the desert. A man who now knew that *I* knew he'd lied to me.

The person who had yet to respond.

"You lied to me about a story." I spoke directly to him. Each word was measured, soft, precise. I implored him to hear me, to actually hear me. To not dismiss my feelings like I feared he might. "A story you admit you don't believe. What else aren't you telling me?"

Joseph's jaw flexed as he held my eyes, and he pushed his glasses up the bridge of his nose. His mouth opened, but before he could answer, a voice spoke up behind me. A butter-and-sugar voice that barely matched the other tones I'd heard from Marinda before. "Why don't you use the weapons?"

I nearly whirled on the witch to remind her to stay out of this conversation when Joseph flinched, his face scrunching as if in pain. What did weapons have to do with anything? Across the table, Seth lowered his head and Oron shuffled on his feet.

Oh. So she wasn't spouting off more nonsense.

I didn't know whether to laugh or cry, wondering when the hits would stop coming. These weapons *were* something interesting. Something they weren't telling me, something that Joseph, at least, had hoped I wouldn't find out about.

Or, at least, hadn't thought relevant for me to know about.

"Well, I see there's another story here," I said, spreading my hands sardonically. I didn't bother concealing the disdain in my voice. "Surprise, surprise."

"As far as we can tell, the weapons are authentic enough." Xi crossed his arms, his hands disappearing up the wide sleeves of his uniform. "Ash created them for his fellow Gods with his own hands. The weapons can only be used by their specific Gods. And they're cursed, meaning they're extremely powerful in their own respects, but with that power comes serious consequences.

"For example, his sword, the weapon of Fire, is nicknamed Lunacy. It gives the bearer unparalleled power over their opponents, but it nibbles away at the wielder's sanity, too." He paused. "It's said that Ash

119

had become quite unstable by the time the Order stripped him of his abilities."

"Ok." I absorbed that information and weighed it with what both Marinda and Kaleal had told me. "What are the other weapons? What can they do?"

Seth tapped the jawbone of his mask. "Earth possesses a sling. Its curse grants the user the ability to spare the lives of others, at the cost of sacrificing someone in their place. Water's trident grants the ability of revival." He glanced at Xi. *The Word* is vague when it references how that works, and we aren't sure if that implies raising the dead… or something else. We haven't uncovered any stories of it being used."

"And, unfortunately, the chakram of Air is likely our best bet." Joseph sighed, running a hand down his face. "It grants the ability to create and strengthen bonds, spread unity, things like that. With its power, in theory, we could reestablish global peace. But that's a no-go."

"What? Why?" I stepped toward him. "Is it the cost? What is the cost of using it?"

Seth waved his hand in a so-so fashion. "It shaves years off the life of the user. The greater the bond the more years."

"A price I'm more than willing to pay—since I'm the one that would have to use it," Joseph quickly added. He looked like he meant it, too. Clearly, this had been a conversation they'd had on more than one occasion.

"Ok, then in that case, where is the chakram?" I asked. "Why don't we use it?"

"We don't know where it is—where any of the weapons are, actually," Pyra admitted. "They've gone missing."

"That's not entirely true," Xi amended. "The artifacts are so indispensable and so powerful that the temples broke them in two. The Order took one part, and each temple kept the other. That was to prevent them from being used, except in dire situations."

Xi reached into a pouch at his hip—one similar to a pouch Pyra wore to hold smoke bombs—and withdrew a piece of metal I recognized as a cross guard for a sword. "We have the pieces of the sling and sword, and, Zara, you've faithfully carried the piece of the trident, which Marinda so thoughtfully saved from the Palace of Oceans."

As I wondered what else he might have squirreled away on his belt, my hand flew to my thigh, to the leather-wrapped base of the dagger. That's why it was shaped so unusually and why it didn't have a true base. It must be one of the trident's prongs. I turned to Marinda, partially in shock. She winked.

"The piece of the chakram is a bit of a mystery, though," Xi said, drawing my attention back to the table. "We recovered the pieces from the ruins of the Air Temple after the Order destroyed it, but it's in bad shape. Our witches *think* it might have retained some of the spell that gives its its power, but we won't know until we can reunite it with its other half."

My heart leaped, then plunged heavily. "But we can't do that because we don't know where the pieces of the weapons in the Order's custody went."

"Exactly." Joseph sighed, shoved his fingers against his eyes, and rubbed. "We've ransacked the campus and every other temple, military establishment, and embassy we can think of searching for them, but they're gone. Not so much as a hint of where they might be."

I wondered when it would stop hitting me so powerfully, the ripples cast by my decision now doubling back on me. If I'd been here, I might have already known all of this. I would have been part of these operations. I could have done my part to help.

Hindsight is such a nasty bit of work, isn't it? Kaleal lounged against a wall in my mind, hair curling over one golden-toned shoulder. *So many what-ifs, so many questions, and none of the relief that comes with answers. I mean, had you stayed here, it's entirely possible that witch's curse*

121

would have destroyed magic as we know it before any of you had a moment to react. She tapped her chin. *My, my, which course of action resulted in the best outcome? We will never know.*

She was right. I didn't want to hand it to her, but she was right. I couldn't waste time wondering about what-ifs. What I could control was the here and now. I could control the choices I made and hope they were the best ones.

"And Geoffrey didn't know anything?" I asked desperately. "If anyone would know where they were... wouldn't it be the Hand of the Gods?"

"We tried that," Joseph said. "Several times. More than several times. He denied it across the board, said he didn't know where they'd vanished after he was sworn in." He rubbed his arm. "He said he didn't particularly care, since he didn't think the Gods would ever amount to anything, especially since he thought at least two of them were dead."

I drew my lower lip between my teeth and gnawed, glancing around the room at the hundreds of empty seats. The people I could see didn't look friendly, but they were intrigued. An idea occurred to me. "Let me talk to him."

Joseph's brow lifted, and I sensed everyone leaning in a little closer. "What makes you think he'll tell you something different?"

"Because things have always been different between us. He's always regarded me as something of a challenge, and he only ever wanted to talk to me, even in the beginning." I nodded, feeling more firm in my idea. "And I spared his life. I could have let him die that day in the tower. I could have finished him off. But maybe..."

"Maybe there's something bigger to come from your mercy." Pyra clapped her hands together. The tension coiling around us snapped like a rubber band and I could breathe again. "For the first time, I'm so glad you didn't destroy that sucker when you had a chance. I like it. Let's give it a shot," she pleaded with Joseph.

He turned from her to me, and I could tell he was wavering in his resolve.

"Come on," I said. "You said it yourself. If we could get the chakram, we could create the bonds of peace that we need. Let me talk to Geoffrey, see if he'll tell me anything. If we do find out the location of the weapons, if we can recover them... maybe we can stop this apocalypse before more people have to die because of it. That way everyone wins."

He turned, scanned the rest of the table.

"Please, Joseph." I squeezed my eyes shut, then finally said the words I hadn't thought I'd ever say. "Give me a few hours to talk to Geoffrey. If I learn nothing, then I'll agree to your plan of seizing the weapons by force—but only if I don't learn anything that can be useful."

Beside me, Pyra jerked, eyes going wide, mirroring Joseph. I saw the moment he finally caved. He had nothing to lose here. Nothing.

"Is that your formal vote?" he asked, motioning to Sonja, who scrambled to pull out her phone.

"It is."

One by one, Sonja went around the room, collecting our votes. Pyra hesitated the longest, mulling over the options, but ultimately relented. Our decision was unanimous.

I didn't wait around to chat afterward. I had a prisoner to see.

Chapter 15

The air whistled as something cut through it—fast. I cupped my hands, rolled on the balls of my feet at the entrance of the security facility, and stopped whatever it was mere centimeters from my back. An apple. A Granny Smith apple, its light green skin shimmery and still damp from a run under the faucet.

"Eat something, would you?" Lach hollered from the shade of an elm tree as he crunched into his matching fruit. "Have I taught you nothing about priorities? There's always time for action and drama, but you'll miss out on it all if you faint because your stomach shriveled up."

"Thanks," I called. The glass door swung open and the fine hairs that framed my face fluttered.

"Next time, eat breakfast."

My eyes narrowed. The elf had an uncanny way of knowing things like that.

Lach took another massive bite of his own apple, not bothering to wipe away the juice that trickled down his chin. His gaze flicked over my shoulder, then back again. "Now go find out something that will save lives."

I tossed the apple high as I slipped through the door before it closed. Inside, I found a lobby as pristine and uniform as the other buildings I'd toured on campus. No muss, no fuss, just a lot of light gray walls, white-tiled floors, and soldiers in camouflage hurrying around.

Most of them went down one of three hallways that branched into the temporary dormitories for visiting troops, but I was most interested in a single doorway. One blocked by a tall, wide fey with a bulldog face and biceps as big as footballs. A badge over his chest proclaimed his last name MORELLI, and I counted the colorful swatches of silk beneath it. I dug around in my pocket and removed a sleek silver card.

The fey's beady eyes scrunched up as I approached, darting from my face to the fruit in my hand, to the three elemental brands visible on my upper left arm. I'd left my jacket behind. He saluted snappily, then snagged my pass and turned it over in his large, weathered hands, checking the markings and signature scrawled on the back.

Morelli turned to a small computer at his elbow but hesitated before running the card across the dancing green laser of the card reader. "Who ya here to see?"

I shifted my weight from foot to foot. "An old friend."

The machine beeped. The fey leaned down, squinting, and whistled. "Geoffrey Marcuzzo." He handed the pass back and reached for the doorhandle at his back. "Didn't he throw you out of the spire or something?"

"Or something." I squeezed the apple. "Our friendship is complicated."

"I'd say." Morelli inclined his head when I walked past him into a hallway more bright and barren than the rest, complete with white walls and harsh fluorescent lighting. "Ms. Ramone, you're only the second visitor he's gotten. Mr. Windrunner used to visit often, but otherwise, he's left alone."

"He's in isolation?" Though a terrible excuse for a human being, I wasn't sure Geoffrey—or anyone—deserved that kind of treatment.

"Sort of. We don't have a ton of prisoners as it is, so things get kind of lonely in general." He scratched at the red stubble sprouting on his cheek. "But Mr. Windrunner wanted him kept to himself, thought it was best for his safety and the safety of everyone else. Mr. Marcuzzo could have filed a grievance, but hasn't complained. A model prisoner, he is, that one."

I turned that information over in my mind. "Thank you, you've been very helpful."

"If you need any help—not that you will, given what you can do—" his chuckle grumbled like rocks rattling in a tumbler— "give us a shout, we'll be watching on the cameras there." He motioned to an orb drilled into the tile of the ceiling in one corner. "Hang a left at the end of the hall. My guy posted there will let you through the door."

The lights buzzed like annoyed hornets as I passed beneath them, reminding me how much I preferred being outdoors. The waxed floors made the rubber of my boots squeak, the sound echoing off the walls. I felt extremely alone, left to my thoughts, and I recalled something TruthTeller had revealed to me about a month ago about Geoffrey: *He would not have been your enemy had you not forced him to take up the mantle.*

I'd come to grips with the words themselves, but I still had questions about what they meant. Hopefully, going straight to the source of my anxiety would help.

As promised, a soldier bigger than Morelli guarded a door at the end of the second hallway. The fey kept one hand on the butt of a rifle slung around his chest as he reached for my pass. He, too, first looked it over, then me, before hitting a button with the point of his elbow. The door buzzed, and he waved me through with the muzzle of his gun.

When the door thudded shut at my back, I shook out my shoulders and moved to the front of the bars, ignoring a short metal bench shoved up against the wall across from them. Inside the cage, with his back propped against the whitewashed cinderblocks, tapping out a rhythm on a kneecap drawn close to his chest, sat my former nemesis.

"You appear to be holding up well," I said. I meant it. Geoffrey seemed healthier, like he'd gotten a solid month's rest. He was also less gaunt and more muscle. He'd grown his hair out, and thick, dark bangs partially obscured the black brands embossed on his forehead—brands that had once sparkled with white light, signaling the return of the Gods.

"Ms. Ramone, I wondered when you would come to see me." His eyes hadn't changed. The overhead lights washed out the gray of one iris and the soft green of the other, but a deep well of pain and knowledge lived in them. It was an expression I was keenly aware of every time I looked in the mirror.

Pop rocks of nerves fizzled in my gut, but I kept my tone light. "I'm told you're a model prisoner."

Geoffrey's chest shook in a silent laugh. He sat upright on the sterile, white sheets, and re-settled his back against the other corner wall so he faced me straight on. His legs dangled over the edge of the twin-sized mattress. "It's difficult to be anything but in here. My mattress is firm, the room quiet. They bring me books and food." He held up a remote. "And I can watch the latest antics you former charges of mine are cooking up whenever I want. Causing trouble would *bring* me trouble, hardly a fair exchange since you restored my sanity."

And spared your life.

I nibbled my chapped lower lip and dug my nails into the delicate flesh of the fruit I still held tight.

I hadn't lied to the other Gods and council members earlier. I could have watched him bleed out when I'd returned to the rooftop of the spire that day. My friends told me they wouldn't have blamed me if I'd chosen to end his life then and there. Geoffrey had brought me so much pain: from his decisions to destroy the temples to killing my friends and family, to chasing me all around the globe until he forced me to fight him head-on.

Part of me felt, had he bled out, justice would have been served. Instead, I'd healed him.

The other Gods and I stripped him of his powers—which he claimed were driving him insane—and we'd forced him to stand trial. He would never see the outside of a jail cell again, but he was seeing the jail cell, which was something.

"How is the silence?" I asked.

Before we'd left Rome for Geneva, he'd slipped me one note: *thank you for the silence.* It was the same silence I'd come to appreciate myself when I'd found a temporary reprieve from Kaleal's taunts, thanks to Lee's help.

Geoffrey tapped his head. "Wonderful. It's nice to feel in control of my mind. I'm much less murderous these days, in case you were wondering." His dark gray shirt bunched around the waist as he leaned forward. "It's not like you to make small talk. Ask me what you've come here to ask."

Everyone thought they knew me so well. Ridley had said something similar when we'd first met, about adapting to my directness. I flipped the apple again. "Where are the weapons?"

"What weapons?"

"Don't play coy with me. I know you know where they are."

He steepled his long fingers beneath his chin. "Even if I knew where those cursed things were, why should I tell you? I may have accepted I made the wrong call seventeen years ago when I destroyed my own temples to stop my vision of the world's end from coming true, but those weapons are still dangerous."

I tucked the apple between my arm and my side and scrubbed at my face. TruthTeller's claim spiraled through my thoughts again, and I lowered to the ground, legs folded. "Because I'm finally ready to listen."

Geoffrey peered at me from the bed, calm and silent like I'd only seen him once before.

What I'd said was a huge departure from the girl I'd been at the start of this all. I used to be all reckless action and immediate decisions. Now I had time. A sliver of it, but enough of an opening to work with. He gripped the side of his mattress and levered himself over, joining me on the ground. Only several silver bars and a few feet of tile separated us.

"Very well, then." He scratched an itch beneath his right eye. "What do you know of the vision the Gods gave me depicting the end of the world?"

"I know it had to do with nuclear fallout, but I can't remember the rest."

He nodded, then motioned at my apple. "Eat, you're far too thin." He waited for me to take an obliging bite.

"When I came into my own in the Order, the Gods blessed me with an image of the trouble you would face, the problem you needed to solve. It was supposed to help me guide you on your path to stopping that devastation." Geffrey rubbed his arms. "But my first vision wasn't of the nuclear bombs going off. I first saw *you* holding the trident with the other Gods behind you, elements in hand—literally—standing on a mountain. You were fighting forces I couldn't see. But you, Zara, you slammed the trident into the ground and the first nuclear bomb went off. I saw *you* ushering in the world's final moments. And you used the weapon of your temple to do it."

I turned that over in my mind.

I understood how, based on what he said, Geoffrey could think we Gods were the ones to blame. That we'd finally turned on the rest of the world. It was also interesting that in his vision I used the trident—when we were convinced the chakram was the best weapon we had in our arsenal. However, I couldn't imagine how the power of revival would have helped anyone in this circumstance. Maybe someone got hurt along the way and needed help?

"But what if I was using the weapon to stop the bombs?" I asked. "Or maybe I was fighting another enemy while we used another of the weapons to stop the bombs. Couldn't that also have been true?"

Geoffrey leveled a look at me. "Of course. But I was also seventeen and naïve, with a chip on my shoulder the size of a Jeep. I didn't see that side of things when I called to attack the temples and eliminate the threat I believed to be was you. It wasn't until years later, and a great deal of reflection, that I concluded I should have waited. I acted impulsively nearly two decades ago, and I'm still paying for those decisions today."

I couldn't stop the question, couldn't hold it back any longer. I needed to know. "So when we met, you didn't want me dead? When you asked me to meet with you?"

My swim team had died immediately after that conversation, and Finn had barely saved me from a similar fate. When I'd later told him of the vision, Finn revealed the Order had it out for the Gods, that they'd always wanted us dead. From there, we'd gone on the run.

"No, I didn't want you dead." Geoffrey sighed. "I didn't handle our conversations like I should have, and those could have cleared a lot of things up. However, at the time I also wasn't aware my second-in-command was actively betraying me and had issued his own orders to kill you." He picked at his cuticles, eyes lowered. "The hotel in Norway, the ambush in Kansas City, the attack on your childhood home—" he ticked off the sites on his fingers— "those were all Toren. Not me. He was telling me one thing and doing another. I did not try to kill you until you tried to kill me."

I set the core of the apple beside me, fingers trembling. TruthTeller was right. I had caused the animosity between us. Geoffrey shouldered his fair share of the blame, but I hadn't helped matters much at all.

If the two of us had bothered to have a civil conversation…

"What a perfect little mess this all is, isn't it?" Geoffrey stretched one arm over his head, his spine popping. "Hindsight really is an ugly mistress."

I jolted involuntarily, recalling how Kaleal had said something similar. "So you clearly saw the weapons being used in your vision. When did you hide them?"

His eyes flicked up and to the right, seeking the camera. "Not long after that. I didn't trust that they wouldn't find their way into the wrong hands."

The iciness of the bars grounded me as I squeezed them, leaning closer. He wasn't denying he'd hidden them anymore. Hope swelled in my chest. I was so close to staving off more war, to preventing a ton of unnecessary deaths. A few more sentences and I'd have the information I needed to present Joseph with the alternative option we all were looking for. "Where are they?"

"In a cavern in a mountain range in China you'll have never heard of." He ran his thumbnail over his teeth. "It's located about seven hundred miles west of the Castle of Glass, but you can't plot it on any map."

"The Order had some witches put a spell on it thousands of years ago, sealing it beneath a force field. Anyone looking at it is spelled to forget whatever they were doing and turn away, forget they ever saw it. Even fey are affected. The only people who can get to it are those who have been there before and the Hand of the Gods. We've periodically added to our stores there over time."

"How convenient." And incredible. The power the Order wielded boggled my mind. I released the bars. My fingers burned as the blood rushed back into them. Something occurred to me. "What else is the Order hiding there?"

The bed creaked as Geoffrey leaned against it, arms banding loosely around his ribs. "A little of this, a little of that. Old artifacts, ancient treasure, things it would rather people forget ever existed." He glanced at the camera again. "It's extremely effective."

My heart elevatored to my throat. "So we need to get to the mountain, find this cavern, and we can get the weapons back."

He chuckled. "You would make it sound so simple. I wasn't finished. The Order doesn't only keep artifacts hidden away in the many peaks of Aldiirin. Fey live there, too, locked inside, banned from leaving forever." He laced his fingers together, spread them wide, and shrugged. "It's a prison for the very worst of the magical kind."

I felt like Rose had landed a flying kick to my chest, and I barely registered the faint unfurling of smoke behind my eyes. It wasn't only *stuff* the Order wanted forgotten… but people, too. I couldn't imagine that fate, to be stuck forever in a place no one knew about, without a way out, forever.

My mouth opened but words didn't come out.

"Yes, I see you're starting to understand the gravity of this situation." Geoffrey leaned his head back on the web of his fingers, chin parallel to the floor. "As you can imagine, the fey hidden away in that mountain range aren't thrilled about being there. So, you have to fight your way through the strays you encounter to get to the caverns themselves. But the mountain range itself… that's another story entirely."

"Don't say it—"

Geoffrey's teeth gleamed in a ferocious smile. "It's cursed, too. Like a labyrinth, the walls of its many canyons constantly shift and change. It's easy to get lost… and crushed."

I dug my thumbs into my eyes so hard that bursts of white light flickered behind my lids. "And let me guess, you can't fly over it."

"Or into it. No flight is allowed whatsoever." Clothing rustled. I opened my eyes as he inched closer to the bars, bi-colored eyes intense, hungry. "Only walking or hiking. And running. Running is important when you've got a group of extremely angry prisoners on your heels."

I scratched the back of my neck, stood. "But it *is* possible to get to the caverns."

Geoffrey answered my rhetorical question. "Yes. It's difficult, but not impossible. I wouldn't have been able to deposit the weapons if it were impossible."

I could work with difficult. The prisoners didn't bother me so much. Regardless of who went on this quest, with the Gods alone, we'd have plenty of firepower. The mountain range itself, however, posed a far bigger problem. I gripped the bars again, pressed my forehead into the space between two of them. Paths shifting unpredictably, in an area that couldn't be mapped, and without the ability to fly out of harm's way easily—that presented a challenge.

"May I ask what you plan to do with the weapons once you find them?"

I glanced at the former Hand. I didn't see the harm in telling him. "We think there's a way to fix the chakram. If we can get it working again, we can use it to establish peace."

"I see." He seemed to mull that over.

"Yeah. Now we need to figure out a way to get through the mountains—"

"I can get you there." Geoffrey stood, too. His hands closed around mine on the bars. The touch made my skin crawl. I stared at them, at the tiny white lines speckling his knuckles, at the pale half-moons of his nails. "I can't draw you a map, but I know the shortcuts through the mountains, I know the pattern of the maze. I know exactly which cavern I'm looking for. I can get you there... as long as you let me accompany you."

I drew back, thoughts swirling, searching for some obvious deception. He claimed he had changed, but he'd brought so much misery when he had been free. I also knew Kaleal lurked nearby, listening to every word, yet said nothing. It worried me.

"Why should I trust you?" I asked.

He reached through the bars as if to touch the oath with the nautical symbols around my bicep, but stopped short. "I know you're familiar with oaths, and you know how seriously the fey take things like life debts. I've always admired that about the fey, and I always felt if I were in the same situation, I'd swear the same." Geoffrey rested the swell of his shoulder against the bars, tucking his head so the camera couldn't see his face. "I may not have sworn an oath, but I owe you a debt for saving my life all the same. I'd like to repay that while I still can."

While I still can. Those words shot like arrows through me.

"Are you dying?" I scanned him with my Iridescence—checking for disease with my Water abilities. "What does that mean?"

"Nothing like that. Call it a sense." He tapped beneath his sternum. "A feeling. I don't know what to make of it, but the end is there, like a shadow, watching me. Waiting."

I stepped back, my heel knocking the core of the apple across the room. "Alright. I'll take it up with the group." Though I had a feeling I knew exactly what they would say. "I can't make you any promises myself, but I'll let you know."

He dropped onto his bed as if he'd expected that answer. "I'll be waiting."

I inclined my head, scooped up the core, and rapped on the door to leave. The soldier opened it as Geoffrey's voice drifted over to me one last time. "And make sure they know I won't help unless you're there. It's you I trust to not kill me, not them."

Chapter 16

"We can't all go." Joseph paced the length of the wall of windows in the library, hands clasped behind his back. He wore the same light blue dress shirt and black slacks from the marathon of television interviews he'd wrapped up about half an hour ago, though he'd slung his jacket over the back of a chair and loosened the marigold tie that accented his eyes.

"That's not true," Pyra protested from her perch atop the grand piano. "Let's all go. Make a day of it. Killing rogue fey, solving a maze, seizing the treasure, it'll be the perfect bonding experience."

I traded a look with Oron, or I assumed I did anyway, because while he'd removed his bone mask, a second mask of black spandex still obscured his features. We exchanged wishy-washy hand gestures, and I grinned as the God of Air rounded on Pyra.

"Because someone needs to hold down the fort, that's why." He batted at her foot, which she pulled back before he made contact. "And get your feet off the furniture. Has no one taught you manners?"

Pyra bobbed in place while cleaning beneath her nails with a dagger. "They tried to, but when I gutted my third etiquette teacher, the temple decided cleaning up the blood and gore wasn't worth it anymore."

"That's a bunch of nonsense if I've ever heard it," Oron signed.

The Fire God pointed at him with her dagger. "Is that a challenge?"

"Stop acting like a petulant child." Xi shot Pyra a parental look of sharp disapproval. Her bottom lip plumped, but she slipped to the bench without protest.

I'd taken half an hour to process everything Geoffrey had told me before calling everyone together to discuss our options. Joseph made us wait to talk until after he finished making the rounds on international news, explaining our decision as best he could. He'd told us to gather in the library because, in his own words, no one ever used it. And, aside from a minor freak out involving a tornado and some projectile books when Joseph discovered Geoffrey had lied to him, everyone had taken the information about the location of the weapons fairly well.

"I'll stay behind and deal with the media." Joseph dropped into an armless wooden chair, the windows at his back. Finn moved so he stood beside him, a small vee forming between his brows. Joseph continued, "I'm already the face of the Order. It wouldn't look right if I up and left now. I'm also hearing some murmurings of nations looking to restart negotiations, which can only help in our favor."

He rubbed his hands together. "And since I'm the only one who can wield the weapon, this gives us time to think, to get it sealed back together here in the safety of Order Headquarters, and make sure everything goes according to plan. The last thing we need is to take rash action in the middle of the mountains."

That sounded like a fine plan to me.

Then he continued, "I also think Zara should stay behind."

I leaned forward, and the leather of my recliner squeaked. "Why should I stay?"

"Because you're the First, and, as you've said a few times now, you've made valuable connections out on the road," Joseph replied. Oh, how I hated having my own words used against me. "You staying here would help me make the case we're serious about finding a viable solution."

He glanced down, tugged at a thread that had unraveled from his sleeve. "And don't hate me for saying this, but I still have some questions about Geoffrey's vision with the trident. I don't see how it could be of much use unless someone's dead, but I'd rather not take the risk if we don't have to."

Seth nodded from his position at one of the windows. The viciously bright sunlight washed out his mask, casting him in silhouette. "I agree. It seems like an unnecessary complication. Pyra and Oron can handle the mountain fine by themselves."

Maybe they're wondering whether you're the True God, after all. Kaleal twisted a ring on her finger. I didn't recognize the light green stone, nor could I recall her wearing jewelry before. *They don't want to chance you getting your hands on that trident.*

It's possible. We'd graduated from terse squabbles to minor, civil conversation since the vote, but I still wished she would stop sounding so reasonable, voicing things that sounded so much like me. *But Joseph sounded adamant earlier when he called your words a story.*

Please. She waved her hand, sending shimmering sparkles across my mind. *The seeds of doubt have already been planted.*

"I agree with your concerns," I said. Joseph turned back to me, face twitching with surprise. Staying behind also came with the added benefit of getting some time away from the rest of the gang to try to repair my relationship with Joseph. "But in case you've forgotten, Geoffrey said he won't go if I don't go. And since he's the only one who knows where we're going... that defeats the whole purpose."

"If Zara goes, then I go." Pyra launched herself across the room and leaped into the chair beside me, shoving me over with a violent motion that made the chair rock side to side. "She left me behind once, she's not doing it again. Plus, we're fire buddies."

"I don't know what that means." I attempted to separate our bodies, but she snagged my elbow in the crook of hers and plastered herself against me. "But I'm not about to argue."

"If they're going, then Oron must go, too."

Pyra and I turned to Seth as one, her body stiffening ever so slightly. Good, it wasn't only me that suspected something was off with him, then.

Joseph unbuttoned the top two buttons of his shirt. "Why? Why do three of us four need to go?"

"When I last checked, Zara couldn't control the Earth. Considering we're heading into the mountains, it's a skill that will come in handy," Seth said. He had a point—even if he didn't include he was a control freak who wanted to have his own player in the game.

Joseph's shoulders slumped, a shadow crossing his face. "Yeah, I guess that makes sense—"

"No, hold on a second. This is ridiculous." I peeled away from Pyra and stood. I couldn't take that forlorn expression on his face, the realization that Joseph was going to be left behind yet again. It was what had gotten me into this mess in the first place, and I'd be damned if I made the same mistake again.

"If the three of us are going, then surely Joseph can take a few days away from his responsibilities, too." I waved my hand dramatically, as if that would help me find the right words. "Joseph, don't you have people who we pay to talk to leaders of other nations?"

He tapped his fingers together. "I mean, yes—"

"These are yes or no questions." I didn't allow him to elaborate. "And don't we have people who know how to negotiate? And people who can handle the press? And soldiers who will keep the Order from being overrun while you're busy for a few days?"

He nodded at the end of each of my sentences. However, the wrinkle between his brows lingered, despite his dawning hope. "I mean, someone still needs to take care of things—"

"Joseph, do you think Seth and I are placemats?" Xi strode forward. "Seth has stood by your side these past few months and I've helped Pyra and Oron. That aside, we both have decades of experience under our belts maintaining large, complicated governmental bodies. I dare say we'll manage for a few days while you tackle tasks that require your specific talents."

The God of Air shook his head, flummoxed, but he said nothing.

"Great." I rounded on the rest of the group, not giving Joseph an opportunity to collect the whirlwind that was his thoughts and raise any more doubts. "It sounds like the Order won't burn to the ground if Joseph goes with us. And if the world goes up in nuclear smoke while we're trekking through the mountains, then I guess there wasn't anything we were going to do to prevent it, anyway."

"You're being a hair flippant," said Xi, "but I see your logic. Besides, if Joseph comes with, then you can fix the chakram on the spot—or see if it's fixable, anyway. Then we can take immediate action, rather than waiting."

Finn was positively beaming beside the awe-struck Joseph, who looked like he couldn't quite believe what he was hearing.

"One more thing and then I'll sit down." I heaved a sigh and produced my dagger. "I know there are concerns about the trident and the role it plays in all this, so what if I leave this behind? If I don't have it, then I can't put the two parts together."

"I think that's a fantastic idea," Oron signed. "I'd go so far as to say we should only bring the half of the chakram we do have. The remaining bits of the sword and the sling can also stay here, safely locked away. We'll bring back the other pieces, but if everything goes according to plan, we shouldn't need to use them."

Part of me doubted that was what Seth would have suggested, but the rest of us jumped on board with the plan too quickly for him to counter. What followed was a messy discussion over how many troops Fire and Earth would each bring, since there would be strength in numbers depending on how many rogue fey we encountered.

Pyra suggested roping the pixies into the mix, arguing Rose would be a valuable asset. While it would have been nice having her guard my back, because few fought more fiercely, in my opinion, than the pixies, I worried about how the lack of aerodynamics would play on their skills and opted for them to stay behind.

Earth and Fire finally agreed on a dozen soldiers each. Among Fire's troops was a witch who would help weld together the chakram. I refused to back down until Ryder and Lach were allowed to tag along, arguing they'd find some way to follow us if we didn't. And Joseph pushed for Finn to join us, bringing our total to a little over thirty. It was the best compromise we could have hoped for.

"Ok." Joseph rose and clapped his hands twice. "We all leave in two days. Be ready or be left behind."

It didn't bypass me he hadn't frowned once after it became clear he was going to join us. In fact, he held himself taller, straighter, a little prouder. It made me feel a little better, and a little more hopeful, for it.

Chapter 17

I offered Finn a towel as he emerged from the river that ran along the west side of Order Headquarters, right outside of the barricaded wall. "Have a good swim?" I asked.

Water scented with secrets streamed from his hair, dripped from his chin, and sluiced in rivulets down his flat stomach before getting caught in his low-hanging swim trunks. He shot me a funny look, then glanced at the migrants crowding the opposite side of the river, watching us intensely, and shook his hair out like a dog before accepting the towel.

"What are you doing here?" he asked. "I thought Joseph had interviews lined up for you all morning long. We may be leaving tonight, but I swore he said he was going to keep every one of you busy up until the last moment."

He bent over, massaging the towel into his hair. Finn was correct. I had interviews lined up. Eleven of them. But I'd needed to see him first. There was something I needed to tell the kelpie before the chaos of the day swept us away.

Finn's hands stilled, and when he removed his towel, his hair stuck up in spikes every which way.

I grinned. "You look like the punk rocker you pretend to be."

He rolled his eyes and snagged a red bag made of windbreaker material off the rocks along the shore. The kelpie slung it over his shoulder and turned back to the high walls of the Order. "How did you know I was here, anyway?"

I followed a half-step behind as we trudged back to the heavily reinforced gate guarded with armed fey soldiers. "Rose may have mentioned a crowd gathers here at dawn every day, hoping for a hint of horseflesh. I figured there was only one horse I knew of daring enough to go for a swim regardless of the danger at our gates." I flicked my thumb back at the hundreds of faces. "Literally."

Finn ignored me. The towel joined the bag over his shoulder. "I'm surprised the guards let you out. It took me months for the tretorraq—" he referenced the hatchet-headed fey with a heaping of defensive magic who typically guarded the city's twenty-foot-high walls— "to warm up to me, and I still have to bribe them with rumors and honey to get outside."

I wiped some grit from the corner of my eye and held my hand a few feet off the ground, palm lowered. A tiny tornado formed between my palm and the ground. I heard some whoops from across the water and grinned. "Did you think Joseph was the only one lucky enough to control Air?"

He matched my smile. The chill in the spring air had done little to dry him off, but he didn't appear all the uncomfortable. Finn inclined his head toward the wall. "Well then, would you help a friend out? I'm at a bit of a disadvantage here."

"Can that wait a moment?" I rocked back on my heels. I didn't want to go back inside yet, where I could feel the walls closing in around me, the weight of my responsibilities pinning me like a butterfly to a board. "There's something I need to tell you."

I'd felt so at ease a moment ago. Now jitters scaled the lining of my stomach.

The amusement on Finn's face faded, though his green eyes twinkled with lingering curiosity. "Well, in that case." He pulled a lump of black fabric from his bag and pulled the shirt over his head, smoothing it across the front of his body. "Does here work? In front of them?" He motioned at the people too far away to hear us. "Or did you have another venue in mind?"

"Here's fine." I didn't mind the onlookers, but I increased the strength of the wind to cover up the sound of our voices. I flipped a flat rock the size of a mouse pad over with my toe, making sure the words about to come out of my mouth were the words I truly wanted to say.

"I'm sorry, Finn. I'm sorry about the other day when I lost my shit and flipped out on you." I peered up at him, squinting through the harsh yellow of the sun rising over the stone walls. "I'm sorry for putting you in a terrible position, forcing you to choose me or Joseph. That wasn't right of me and I was a horrible friend."

My glance cut away, skirted the frothy bubbles ribboning around the rocks jutting from the river, and returned to Finn's face. "That was incredibly self-centered of me, but I promise I learned from it. I feel horrible about what I did and I won't do that again."

Finn stared at me with an expression so solemn the jitters in my gut transformed into full-on tremors I was positive measured on the Richter scale somewhere. I fought the urge to cross my arms, to ball up my body defensively, and left myself wide open, accepting of whatever was going through his thoughts. He looked positively pissed.

Nothing could have surprised me more when Finn finally said, "That was—thank you, Z. You didn't need to say that, but I'm glad you did."

The churning in my stomach stilled, the turbulence vaporizing instantly. I felt like I'd been trudging through endless mountains of snow for days and finally took a moment to stop and relax, to remember what it was like to not move.

I blinked up into his face, into the soft moss of his eyes. "So we're good? You and me? Because I've been sick with worry the past day thinking I might have—"

He put his hand on my arm, right over the elemental brands, and squeezed. "Of course we're good. Sure, you got a little too caught up in your emotions, but don't forget, I know you." Finn a step back on the smooth rocks. "That's what you've always done. I don't think you could have defeated Toren's army if you hadn't gotten a little caught up in the moment. I appreciate your apology, so don't sweat it anymore."

I threaded my fingers through the loose loops of my braid, the gears in my mind turning. The clouds shifted across the sky and the slash of deep red across the horizon lightened to a subtle, blushing rose. Almost time to get back for my first interview.

"You're different now," I observed. "A good different, but still different."

"How do you mean?" he asked.

"You used to be so snarky, always with the quips and the sarcastic jabs. Now you're…" I motioned to him, hands moving up and down. "It's like you're more settled. Like you've finally made peace with whatever has been haunting you and you're finally… living."

"Don't tell me Ryder and that Lachlan guy don't keep you on your toes with the comebacks," Finn said with a smirk. Then it faded, and he toyed with his eyebrow piercing. Finally, he lifted one shoulder. "I dunno. I think I have grown up a little. Some of it was the constant fighting—you guys seriously needed someone to tell you when to buckle down, or I don't know if we would have ever made it to the Lost City and found Oron."

He sighed, a small, secret smile tugging at his lips. "I think some of it was Joseph—maybe a lot of it was Joseph. He's so incredibly passionate in such a cerebral way. He shouldered all this responsibility without hesitation or complaint, he's grown into this leader in every definition of the word… and I think being here for that ride made me reevaluate my life, too."

I listened to the gusting wind, the murmuring of the growing crowd across the way. "I'm happy for you." And I was. "It's a good look for you."

He threw his head back and laughed. "Now I need you and Joseph to make amends. You guys are such crazy passionate people in such totally opposite ways. It will be interesting to see what amazing things you'll dream up when you finally put your heads together."

I didn't know what to say when it came to Joseph. I owed him an apology, too, but something about that felt a million times more monumental than apologizing to Finn—and that had taken every single one of my nerves to pull off.

"Like I said before, don't sweat it." Finn read my thoughts as clearly as if I'd spoken them out loud. "You already took a fantastic first step, making sure he joined us on the trip. I know he appreciated it was you who spoke up for him yesterday. It'll take some time, but as long as you don't force anything, I know you two will figure things out."

I drew my lip between my teeth, my magic jumping in my fingertips.

"But, in the meantime, you have interviews you need to get to." Finn rounded on me and gave me a firm shove toward headquarters. "And missing even one of those will not endear you to my dear boyfriend."

"Yeah, yeah." With Finn's hand in mine, I shot us to the top of the wall beside a pair of scowling soldiers. I could practically hear their teeth grinding in frustration at my antics. Behind us, the crowd shouted its approval of the demonstration.

I grinned and turned, releasing more of my magic, giving them a small show on the water as thanks for leaving us be so we could talk, before trotting to catch up with Finn as he jogged down the wall and back into the compound once more.

Chapter 18

The next day, Ryder glared up at the blue-tinted mountaintops in the distance as if they'd personally insulted him. Overhead, the twin engines of the plane that had brought us here trailed streams of white as it left us. Xi had recommended the pilot stay at the Fire Temple for a few days while we trekked through the mountains. He didn't want a random plane in a field drawing undue attention.

"I don't like this," the incubus growled.

"I don't think any of us like this." I crouched among the pastel wildflowers and soft grass that rose to my knees as far as I could see. I wasn't sure why we'd stopped here, exactly. The nearest mountains were miles away... but I figured that had something to do with the Order's illusion.

My bigger and more immediate priority had been finding water. I'd worried on the flight over when I hadn't seen many winding rivers or glimmering ponds from the window of the plane. However, once we'd landed, I'd sensed a massive lake north of here, large enough to supply me with plenty of ammo should I need it. "That's the point."

"Oy, speak for yourself." Lach tossed me my pack and I caught it before it beaned me in the head. "I think we're going to have a blast."

"Literally." Pyra tapped powdery ash from her cigarette. "Don't forget: it's not only getting in that's difficult. We have to get out, too."

"That's what she said," Lach cackled. He dodged a swipe from Ryder who couldn't hold back his smirk, and sprinted past a half-dozen Fire troops double-checking their gear. Butterflies with orange and black wings erupted into the skies as he disrupted the grass.

"Where did you pick him up, anyway?" Pyra cradled her last inhale of smoke in her lungs for a few seconds, then blew it out through her nose. It curled around her face in ways that reminded me of Shu's whiskers. "The two of you couldn't be less alike if you tried."

"I thought you were quitting," I said with a pointed look at the Fire God as she snubbed out the cancer stick on the metal center of a throwing star.

She cocked an eyebrow at me. "Yes, quitting. Present tense. I allow myself one smoke when I'm stressed out."

"I see," I said, though I didn't.

Pyra swiped at the front of her vest a few times. "Now to my much more important question, but do you and that weirdo share anything in common? Inquiring minds want to know because you two don't make sense."

Satiny petals brushed the backs of my hands as I braced them on my knees and stood, brushing powdery pollen off my black shirt and blue jeans. "We both see a job that needs finished and see it through. Sometimes that's enough."

"Ah, boss, you're gonna make me cry." Lach flung an arm around my neck and dragged me against him. He pressed his nose to my hair, sniffling wetly.

"Do you have a cold?"

"Nope, I'm plenty warm thanks to your beautiful words."

Something wet slicked across my ear, and I shoved at his chest. "Did you lick me?" I brushed the spot and stared at my hand. "You seriously licked me. What is wrong with you?" I slammed a ball of water into the back of the elf's head, knocking his hat clean off, and Ryder tripped him when he tried to run. "I swear. You are such a child."

Pyra fell over, laughing as Oron watched the scene with hands braced on his hips, head tipping back and forth. Beyond them, Joseph and Finn poured over a map. The former scratched his head miserably as he glanced from the page to the mountaintops and back again.

"He's an excellent addition to your team," Geoffrey murmured as he came up beside me.

"Who? Joseph?" I asked. "He's been here. I swear you've ignored him at least a half dozen times today alone, though."

Geoffrey grunted and moved his bag more firmly up on his shoulder. "No, that elf of yours." He fixed his attention on the group of soldiers preparing their gear. "You needed someone who made you laugh. You'll need that inside Aldiirin."

"Sure." It freaked me out, seeing Geoffrey amongst us wearing regular clothes. For as long as I'd known him, he preferred long robes and black button-up shirts. Today, however, he wore a pair of tan cargo pants and a green, long-sleeve shirt that softened everything about him, solidifying his status as a human amongst all us Gods and fey. He ran his hand over his newly cropped hair, nails sifting through the longer locks on top and scratching the shorter trim on the sides. He seemed so... normal. It wasn't right.

Ryder noticed the former Hand standing beside me and strode over. The air around him shimmered with a faint black hue I assumed was his magic, but imagined was his hostility taking physical shape.

Geoffrey dipped so his lips were level with my ear. "Him, though, I'm not so sure about."

"The feeling's mutual," grumbled the incubus. Despite the talons sprouting from his fingers, his grip felt remarkably light as he tugged me from Geoffrey, cocooning me against his chest. "I don't trust you. You don't trust me. The only reason you're alive now is because of her, and the same goes for your continuing status as a living, breathing human being here on forward."

"Charming." Geoffrey lifted a brow at me in an I-told-you-so way before turning to the group. He brought his fingers to his lips and released a shrill whistle. "Everyone, wrap up your final checks. We'll be heading out in a few minutes." And he beelined for the Earth troops dressed in shades of brown who were wrangling the last of their stuff into a few bags.

"I really don't like that guy," Finn said. He and Joseph had sidled up beside us while Ryder and Geoffrey traded jabs. The kelpie kept his eyes on Geoffrey and crossed his arms across his chest. "Something about him feels off."

Everyone feels off, I wanted to say, but held my tongue. The vibes I got from Geoffrey didn't compare to the weird energy I picked up from the Earth troops. The rest of us also seemed... edgier than normal.

"Geoffrey has always been off," Ryder agreed. He rubbed his hands up and down my arms through my jacket. I settled against him, enjoying the sensation. "Zara, I want you to stay with either me or Finn until we're putting this mountain in our rearview mirror. And I'm not negotiating with you."

I tipped my head back to glare at him, but didn't argue. It wasn't in me. I agreed with him on this one. Finn and Ryder had always had my back.

"I'll pretend I didn't hear that insult," Lach called over to us. "I had her back when neither of you were anywhere to be found. Besides, the kelpie here's got his own God to worry about."

The elf didn't sound as committed to the argument like he normally was with Ryder, and I pulled away from the incubus, seeking him out. A few yards away, Lach frowned deeply as he dug around his bag, movements jerky until he found whatever it was he was hunting for and his shoulders relaxed. As if sensing my attention, he motioned me over.

I glanced up at Ryder, who lifted his brows but shrugged, and I wandered over to the elf. At my back, Ryder asked Joseph if he could look at the map he'd brought. Apparently, the God wasn't the only one confused about what we were doing here.

"Are you ok?" I asked Lach, allowing him to turn us so our backs were to the group. "You're acting weird, even for you."

He glanced at me, expression sober, and reached into his bag again. "I brought something for you," he said. With a glance around us, he yanked me to his side, our backs to the rest of the group, pulled something wrapped in cloth from his bag, and dropped it into my pack. Like magic, he was back to his old self, as if carrying whatever that was had been a weight he hadn't wanted to shoulder. "Go ahead. Look. But be careful."

My mouth had gone dry and I couldn't summon any moisture. A huge part of me wanted to throw the bag into the grass and leave it there for the snakes and mice to find, but another part of me, the curious part that always won over my sensible one, peered into the depths. I reached in, found the bundle, and unwrapped it. A hint of blue steel winked back at me.

A roaring filled my ears, and I jammed the weapon deeper into the bag as if that might make it disappear. "What is this?" I demanded, icy tingles racing across my cheeks and down my spine. "What did you do?"

"I stole it back for you," Lach whispered excitedly. "I saw how you looked when Pyra gave you that thing, like she'd gifted you the world. And then I saw how heartbroken you were when they made you give it up and leave it with those other artifacts. I swapped it with another look-alike before they locked it up."

I couldn't feel my arms. Couldn't feel much of anything, actually. The elf hadn't been there, in the library, when we'd discussed our plan, and I hadn't thought to fill him in on it. I hadn't considered the elf would do something this reckless. But no. This fit his character completely.

This treasure would have been too irresistible for his impulsive nature to resist.

I touched numb fingers to my face. "This is bad."

A breath shuddered from my chest. What would everyone think when they found out the blade was here? Would they think I'd lied to them? That I'd asked Lachlan to go behind their backs and steal it back for me?

The plane was gone, so it was too late to hide it on board. And I couldn't risk leaving it here. It was too valuable to abandon for just anyone to find. My thoughts tripped over one another. That meant... though it was the last thing I wanted to do, I'd have to take it with us. I couldn't think of any alternatives.

"This is so very, very bad," I whispered.

The elf seemed to crumple, his earlier delight in doing something he thought I would have appreciated nowhere to be found. "What's wrong?" he asked. "It's yours. And I didn't trust that Earth Temple guy around it. He kept staring at it like he might—"

"You don't understand," I seethed. I wanted to grind him into the ground. I wanted to strike him with a bolt of lightning. I wanted to rail on him like nothing else, but I couldn't risk anyone else knowing what had happened. They would never trust me again.

Joseph would never trust me again.

With effort, I forced my lips to turn upward, forced my body to soften, and I threw the bag over my shoulder. The shape of the dagger fell perfectly between my shoulder blades. "No one can know about this," I said. "I will keep it, but you can't say anything about the dagger. I was supposed to leave it behind at headquarters because there are concerns about what it might be able to do if it's joined with a bigger weapon."

Lach cocked his head. "What kind of concerns—"

"Let's go." A sharp whistle followed Geoffrey's command, cutting

Lach's question off. "Get your things and follow me."

I shot the elf a look, silently commanding him to let it go. To let me handle this. Our conversation was over, and I doubted we would have time to discuss it further at any point from here on out. But at least I had the dagger with me. I still had control over this situation. I couldn't let anyone rifle through my bag, and I couldn't let on that anything was amiss. I still had my silver dagger, the one I'd gotten as a replacement, strapped to my thigh. As long as I wore that one and stayed cool... no one would be the wiser.

I rejoined Ryder, trying to shake the stiffness from my shoulders.

"Everything ok?" he asked without looking up. "You guys seemed a little intense there."

I chewed my lip. Ryder needed to know what had happened, but only him. "Lach switched the daggers and brought mine with him. I've got it now, but we can't let anyone know we have it."

Though his expression remained pleasant, I felt his magic snap, his temper flare. He didn't say anything for a long minute, his gaze flicking across the field. "Make sure no one else knows you have it. It's a complication, but not an insurmountable one."

"Agreed."

I gripped the straps of my bag tighter, and together we joined the rest of the group where they congregated around Geoffrey in the field. Ryder threw his arm around my back casually, but protectively, making his stance on the situation clear. If anyone else found out about the truth of the weapon and confronted me about it, they'd have to go through him first.

"Where, exactly, are we going?" Joseph grumbled. He had yet to look my way, but I wasn't picking up on any fresh waves of hostility. The God sometimes used his abilities to listen in on conversations from far away, but I took his lack of reaction to mean I'd muddled my discussions enough to not pique his interest.

The former Hand offered a lopsided grin that didn't match his chilly eyes. He pointed to a large boulder that he'd directed the pilot to land beside earlier. It stood about ten feet tall and was maybe twenty feet wide. "You wanted to know where the entrance to Aldiirin was. That's one of them. That rock marks one of the only three ways in and out. The only way through is if I give you permission to follow me."

In fascination, our group trailed him to the rock. Joseph appeared to be the most skeptical as he inspected the black and brown speckled stone. "Explain."

"Nah." Geoffrey turned. "Just follow my lead."

And he promptly walked into the boulder and vanished.

Chapter 19

L ach blew on his hands and rubbed them together. "Is it me, or is it about fifteen degrees cooler in here than it was outside of the barrier?" he asked, pretending like everything was normal between us.

Even with my magic warming my blood, I'd noticed the dip in temperature the moment we'd entered Aldiirin. I still couldn't wrap my mind around what had happened. One moment we'd been in a sunny field surrounded by flowers and the next we were deep in the center of a densely wooded area at the base of a massive mountain. Beyond it stretched more intimidatingly tall peaks, dark with foliage that shouldn't have grown on rocks that high up.

Here at the bottom, the pine trees bunched together like matchsticks in a box. Dead branches stuck out in odd angles from their trunks, making it difficult to move between them. Their tall, triangle peaks swayed precariously in the snapping, unrelenting wind that sent icy chills ripping right through our clothes. That wind, too, hadn't existed on the outside of the barrier, and Joseph had already grumbled about not being able to control the gusts like he should have.

He wasn't the only one affected by whatever strange magic was at play here. Thick, dark clouds hung low overhead, periodically obscuring the tops of the mountain peaks and blocking out the sun. I'd tried every trick in my book to whisk away the thunderheads, to no avail. Instead,

I barely held off the rain that threatened.

Geoffrey wiped his forehead with his sleeve, smearing black mud across his skin, and held back a branch so the rest of us could pass. "The original Order wanted to make this place as miserable as it could. What you're encountering now is only the beginning."

"I see why you hate this guy so much," Lach mumbled to me. "He's always spouting off some fun fact that makes me want to stab him."

After a beat, I accepted his reaching grasp, and the elf hauled me up the seven-foot width of another fallen log. My stomach dropped when I lost my foothold, but Finn was there, holding my legs as he shoved me up.

"Add in the fact he's always trying to kill one of us, and you've got a pretty solid picture," the kelpie said. His emerald eyes glowed faintly as he pushed Joseph up after me. I wondered how close he was to transforming into his demon-horse form. Surely four legs and a bigger body would have been more useful right about now. I assumed he held off because of the energy it would take to hold his form.

The five of us had opted to bring up the rear, and Ryder stood with his back to us, shoulders rising and falling as he panted, eyes keen as he both kept Geoffrey in his line-of-sight while also monitoring for danger. An hour in and we hadn't heard or seen much. It felt eerie; the silence lacked the most minor trill of birds and hum of insects. Nothing about this mountain was natural.

Beside me, Joseph sat and pulled out a notebook. It had been blank when we'd started, and he'd already filled a dozen pages with his observations, scribbling in tiny script similar to the stuff I'd given up trying to decipher in my search to eradicate the curse killing the daemoni. His lips moved silently as he quickly sketched a leaf and added a notation about the smell of this place.

It was incredibly damp here, and we couldn't out-pace the scent of wet moss and rotting wood.

I cast out my senses as Ryder dispersed into mist and used the wind currents to drift up the side of the log. All fey could detect the signatures of other magical creatures as long as they weren't shielded, but I preferred to use my Water abilities since people were seventy percent water. Not only was my reach farther, but I could use it more accurately.

Behind us, I picked up on a few rabbits and squirrels, something that felt like a deer.

"I wouldn't mind being blasted with a fireball right about now." Lach nudged my arm with his elbow. "At least I'd be warm as I burned alive."

"I don't think that's how it works," I murmured, distracted. I backtracked to the deer, trying to get a sense of its signature, but it had disappeared. I drew some of my energy away from the storm clouds, expanding my senses farther, looking for it again, when I stumbled across several more figures. Smaller, yet packed with magic. The prisoners had found us.

I'd barely opened my mouth to warn the others when a man screamed.

On a bed of pine needles, partially obscured by a tree, one of the Earth soldiers collapsed, an arrow through his chest. Blood pooled thickly around him as his fellow soldiers fanned out, seeking protection behind the dense trunks. Finn shouted as another arrow whizzed past his head, and he shoved Joseph and me off the log, tumbling quickly after. I nearly cracked my head on a rock, but rolled in time and scrambled back up, scouring the trees. This low to the ground, I couldn't see anything except—

I felt the arrow before it hit home, but Joseph beat me to the punch, knocking it away with a flick of his wrist. He answered my nod of thanks with one of his own, keeping his back smashed against Finn's as they scanned for danger. I mentally tracked the trajectory of the arrow to a fey whose head was topped by an impressive set of antlers. His naked torso tapered off into a stag's body. One cloven hoof scraped the dirt as he flexed his arms, and another arrow darted my way.

Pyra disintegrated it with a shout, flames roaring up around her as she rushed to engage the enemy.

Ryder dropped in front of me. "Frode. Maybe two dozen of them, all stags and all armed. That'll be tricky." He glanced over my head at Finn. "Some elves and trolls, too. They've got us surrounded."

Finn shifted into his second form, his dark hide littered with rotting seaweed, his backward-facing hooves pawing at the ground. Joseph swung onto his broad back and gripped Finn's sides with his knees, a ball of super-fast wind swirling between his hands. The God unleashed his powers as Finn sprinted past me, charging at one of the approaching frode with a whinny that nearly pierced my eardrums.

Lach landed in a crouch beside me, TruthTeller strung and clasped firmly in his grip. He flipped his hat around and scanned the trees. "I can get the trolls at our back as long as you hold off the stags."

"Need any magic?" I asked, falling into familiar step with him, dragging the strands of my three elements forward. Somewhere through the trees, metal sang against metal as the Fire soldiers engaged with more of the enemy. A fireball lit up the dusky sky, and I wondered how many Pyra had taken out in one burst.

"I'm good. TruthTeller here is feeling feisty." The elf tapped his head with a two-fingered salute, hooked the bow over his shoulder, and scrambled back up the side of the log again. I heard the telltale twang and a scream that followed when one of his magical arrows found its home in an enemy's chest.

"You and me, glowstick." Ryder pressed a hard kiss to the side of my head. "Do me a favor and don't die."

A loud crack split the air and a trio of pine trees swayed precariously as the ground was ripped out from under them. Several frode fell into the hole Oron had created, their antlers tangling in the veiny roots as they scrambled to escape. They didn't stand a chance when the trees crashed back down, crushing them alive.

Swords clanged and men yelled. The scents of coppery blood mingled with the freshly turned dirt and dead leaves. I left the safety of my log, intent on the half dozen frode firing arrows at a pair of Earth soldiers pinned down behind a tree.

With a snarl, I released my hold on the skies and the clouds relinquished the icy shards of driving rain that had built up in their black bellies. I slashed out, the scent of ozone burning my nostrils as a bolt of lightning scorched one of the frode unfortunate enough to be left out in the open.

I shook out my arms, clutching more magic to myself, welcoming the pounding rain that churned up mud around my feet. One stag noticed my approach and ripped off another arrow. I spliced it in two with my sword of ice and kicked aside the small stone head. I twirled the blade in my hand, then pulled it back, past my ear, and threw it. The blade split into four smaller daggers as it sheared through the rain and air. Three of the frode went down without a sound. The fourth dagger nicked its target, who charged at me, antlers first.

I slammed a foot down, freezing the earth beneath his hooves as he charged down the incline. The fey's legs shot out from under him. His eyes rolled wildly, arms flailing, as he fought for purchase. I didn't watch as he crashed into the trunk of a tree with a sickly crunch.

Mist washed over me as Ryder engaged the remaining two stags, flickering between his real and smoke forms in a wicked dance of death. Icy chills swamped me when one of the fey nearly gored him, but Ryder braced, grabbed the charging fey by the antlers, flipped the creature over his head, and slammed his enemy's body into the ground. The incubus didn't wait for the frode to recover. He snagged a thick tree branch with a sharpened tip off the ground and drove it into the fey's chest. The frode gasped once, blood spilling from the wound, before going limp.

Air surged back into my lungs.

With a sneer, Ryder turned his full attention on the other attacker who had dropped his bow in his rush to retreat. The incubus snatched it up, ripped the string away, and snapped the weapon in half. He threw one of the splintered ends at the fey, who tumbled when the shaft impaled him through the chest. Ryder shook his head at the carnage and wiped blood from his hands onto his pants.

At my back, Lach whooped and boulders tumbled past as Oron launched another assault.

I turned to see what had happened when a body blocked my path. I dropped back, narrowly missing the thrust of a sword.

"Where do you think you're going?" the elf taunted. "Round one is only beginning."

He smiled grimly and flicked blood from his sword as we circled one another. The rain splattered harder, flattening his long hair to the sides of his head. With a sneer, he swiped dripping bangs from his eyes. Lightning flickered, exposing a jagged pink scar that slashed across his face and twisted his lips. Wordlessly, I tucked away my magic and drew my silver dagger—part of me wishing it were another dagger tucked away in the bag I'd abandoned by the log.

Magic wouldn't help me here.

"What a pity." The elf was short for his kind, almost my height. He clicked his tongue, footing remarkably even in the mud and tangled roots. "I so hoped you'd blast me with some of that delicious fire, too. Maybe next time."

"I didn't know you could fight if you were cut into pieces." I launched myself at him, dagger cracking against his sword with a ringing clang that sang up my arm. The vibration shook so badly, I nearly dropped my weapon, but gritted my teeth and held on. We grappled for a second, drew apart, then clashed again and again. As always against elves, I found myself at a disadvantage. They started training with weapons from the crib, and I had barely six months of experience under my belt.

I tripped over a raised tree root and slipped, trying to find my balance. My dagger flew from my hand and I flipped quickly, barely avoiding becoming a kebob as the elf stabbed downward. I panted, covered in mud, scrambling back until I hit the trunk of the oak that had tripped me up.

In one hand I clutched a rock slightly smaller than my fist, and in the other, I extended a new sword of ice. I didn't want to use it. I wasn't sure if he could absorb my water abilities through the clash of our weapons, but I wasn't about to go down without throwing everything I had at him.

The elf advanced, attention fixed on the icy blade. "Looks like I'll get what I want after all."

I guess that answered my question.

Purple lightning arced through the clouds, followed by a sharp clap of thunder. The scent of burning flesh seared my nostrils. My hair lifted, reacting to the electrical charge of static.

The elf ran at me, but rather than turn and flee like I believed he expected of me, I charged *at* him, fist clenched tight around the rock. He adjusted remarkably quickly, rolling his blade to the side, preparing to swipe it into my side. I dipped, twisted, and popped up, bashing him in the temple. He staggered back, but didn't go down, didn't drop his sword. He shook his head, soaked hair flying in all directions, dazed.

I hadn't hit him hard enough.

"Feisty." He grunted, found his footing. "Let's go again."

As he set his stance, I flexed my fingers, searching for something that might help. Running was out of the question, but I doubted my luck would hold if he tried to run me through with his sword again. I'd escaped unscathed once only because I'd ridden a wave of sheer nerves. My flames roared to life in my belly. Maybe if I hit him hard enough, fast enough, I could bring him down long enough to stab him myself.

Fire scorched my fingertips and the fey leered, eyeing the inferno hungrily. He opened his mouth, took a step forward, then staggered, choking. His sword toppled to the ground. Through his chest, the tip of my dagger had sprouted. Behind the elf, amber eyes swirling and blazing with unholy heat, Ryder twisted the blade before shoving the fey off the weapon. He collapsed face-down in a puddle and didn't move.

"You stabbed him in the back," I gasped, struggling to catch my wind. The fireball engulfing my hand vanished in a puff of steam. "I can't believe you did that."

"All's fair in war." Ryder flipped my dagger, grabbed the flat side of it out of the air with two fingers, and presented the handle to me. "You have to watch your own back. Remember that."

Still reeling, I cast out my senses again but couldn't detect any other signs of fighting. "Is it over?"

"If it helps, the good guys won."

Ryder snagged my hand, dragging me back through the trees. I held fast to him and stumbled over tree roots and dead bodies, squinting at the harsh light visible between the thick trunks. We finally emerged in a clearing where a large fire burned.

The rain had stopped on its own accord, and it seemed Pyra was perfectly content with letting half the forest burn. Gathered around the blaze, and the prone figures of four bodies, stood the rest of our troop. I spotted Finn first, still in his kelpie form, with Joseph at his side. The flat planes of the God's face drawn were tight with fatigue and misery as he watched the leaping flames. Finn released a soft sound when he spotted me, drawing the attention of everyone else.

Off to the side, beneath the branch of a pine tree forming a sort of umbrella, sat Lach. His arm banded around his chest, and he bared his teeth in a grimace. The other Gods appeared to be ok, too, though

Pyra glared at the ground where two of her soldiers lay. The other two belonged to soldiers of the Earth temple.

Geoffrey scanned our somber faces in the glow of the firelight.

"Mourn your dead. Gather your gear, or what's left of it, anyway. We need to keep going," he ordered. He truly was one of the most callous people I'd ever met. "The scent of blood and war will draw more of them, and they'll be better prepared next time. We need to keep moving before they catch up."

Judging by the glowering eyes and the scuffing feet, everyone hated Geoffrey profusely in that moment, but no one argued.

Sometimes the most heartless comments made the most sense.

- - -

"The sun has set."

"No, it hasn't."

"How can you tell?"

"Because it's slightly darker than it was half an hour ago."

"I haven't been able to see my feet for the past hour, what's your point?"

Pyra shut up the sniping of her troops with three sharp blasts of fire. "Enough. Everyone. I'm calling it." She swiveled and jabbed Geoffrey in the ribs with the leather sheath of her dagger. "I don't care what you say. We're done for the day. If we keep going, we won't have to wait for your prisoners to finish us off, we'll die tripping over our own feet."

He held up his hands.

Bloodied and battle-weary, we examined our surroundings. Despite walking all day, little had changed aside from the steady incline of the terrain. Oron's white cloak glowed like a beacon as he prodded a few of his guys and went about setting up tents and rolling out sleeping bags on the damp moss. We'd lost another two men in three more attacks, and exhaustion congealed thickly with our falling spirits.

"Come on." Ryder lifted my bag from my back. "Let's get your stuff set up so you can sleep."

"Are you going to set up my bag, too, Ry?" Lachlan's voice lacked its usual zest as he leaned against a gnarled maple tree. He took off his hat and fluffed his hair. "I'd like a cup of warm milk and a bedtime story, if you're taking requests."

"I'm not." Ryder flattened the blanket, tugged some dead branches out from beneath it, and patted it absently. He reached for my hand. The fact he didn't stand back up proved testament to how tired he was, too. "Come on, lay down. I'll stay with you for a bit before joining the first scouts."

My legs folded, and I dropped beside him, unashamed in how easily I curled against his side. His warmth wasn't necessary, but I needed the comfort he offered more than anything. I stared down at the dark stains on my hands, considered washing away the blood and dirt, but couldn't bring myself to move.

I'd killed fey today. Several of them. Nausea roiled in my gut, but I didn't have anything in it to expel. They weren't my first kills, but taking lives never got any easier.

Fabric flapped, and another blanket dropped to the ground beside mine. I didn't bother looking up. I'd recognized Finn's footsteps as he approached. He offered a piece of jerky, which I took, before he collapsed on his mat. The kelpie draped his arm over his face, and his voice came out muffled. "If you don't eat that willingly, I'll have Ryder hold you down while I force it down your throat."

"Do you talk to Joseph that way?" I asked. I tore off a chunk with my teeth and chewed slowly. Whatever. "I'm surprised he hasn't punched you yet."

Finn's teeth gleamed in the darkness. "Maybe he did."

"Glad to know I'm not the only one who's had to resort to such tactics," Lachlan interjected. He didn't bother spreading out a blanket as he sat beside me. "I don't know how you stayed alive until now without our help."

"I swam. A lot." I pressed myself deeper into Ryder's side, staring out into the blank nothingness of the woods over Finn's prone form. I wondered where Joseph had wandered off to. Maybe he was with Pyra and Oron, making sure the soldiers were settled in.

Ryder worked my sleeve up my arm with one hand and traced the oaths. I promptly forgot about Joseph and practically purred, quietly liking how he'd adopted a habit of mine for himself. "I kept a strict schedule and ate whatever my trainers put in front of me—which was a lot. You needed calories to compete at that level."

"What a dreadful story," Lach murmured and moved so he sat across from me, beyond Ryder's reach. I grinned at him, the feeling foreign on my face, and gnawed on another bite of jerky. "Seriously, you're liable to make small children cry if you keep that up."

"You asked for a story."

"I demand a do-over."

"Do you ever shut up?" Pyra whisper-yelled, joining our group. She crunched loudly on something and took Lach's place beside me while Joseph crept in behind her, quiet as a windless day, and sat beside Finn's prone form. He ran his fingers through the kelpie's hair as he listened to us talk, and part of me melted, seeing how they were with one another.

Pyra dipped her hand into a bag of what I now realized were nuts, and shoved more into her mouth, chewing with her mouth open. "Gods, if I wanted to hear people talk so much I couldn't hear myself think, I would have stayed at the Castle of Glass."

"You know you love it," Lach said. "I've already won you over."

"Fat chance."

Finn released a loud snore. Pyra glanced at me, daring me to keep quiet, but both of us failed and burst into giggles. I should have felt bad laughing when so much ugliness had happened, but I needed the release. I felt Ryder's lips curve where he'd pressed them against the top of my head. Across from me, Joseph's shoulders shook with silent laughter.

"You should take a hint from Finn and get some sleep," Ryder grumbled.

Pyra's hand flew into the air, showering us with nuts. "I call sleeping with Zara."

Lach choked, leaves rustling as he rolled onto his side, sniggering.

"Best way to stay warm," Pyra continued, ignoring him, and jabbed me twice with her elbow. "Ain't that right, fire buddy?"

"Considering you both run the warmest temperatures in the entire camp, that seems counterproductive," said Ryder. "And you're insane if you think I'm giving her up without a fight."

Pyra seemed to think this over. "If I have to lift another sword tonight, my arms are likely to fall off." She tapped her cheek, then cupped a fist in the flat of her hand. "But I do play a mean game of Rock, Paper, Scissors."

Ryder boomed with laughter, waking Finn.

Twigs snapped, and I tensed as Geoffrey approached with Oron at his side. They hovered at the edge of our little group. "Not to interrupt—"

"People who say that are always interrupting." Lach sat upright and removed his needle-like daggers from his sleeve. "If you're going to interrupt, do it. It's less annoying that way."

"Noted," Geoffrey said dryly. "Anyway, we thought we would join you over here. The soldiers appear to be all set up in their camps."

"Have the scouts left yet?" Ryder murmured against my hair. I tensed against him.

"Not yet, but they will be soon."

I didn't want him to go, but I bit my tongue. I'd be ok if he left. It wasn't a huge deal. It wasn't like I needed him with me to sleep.

Sure, like you didn't need him last night or the night before... or the night before that, came a voice inside my head. I wasn't sure whether to attribute it to Kaleal or to myself. They sounded similar these days. And I rarely liked what they had to say.

More leaves rustled as the last sleeping bags were rolled out, but no one slipped between the covers yet, still too high-strung from our earlier battles, on edge in our unfamiliar surroundings. Even Finn was awake, his arm thrown around Joseph's shoulders, his eyes glowing slits in the dark as he stared up at the leaves while listening to the forest settle around us.

When the silence stretched a hair too long and I couldn't stand it anymore, I asked, "Geoffrey, you've had a lot of time to think in prison, right?"

I felt more than saw him nod.

"If there's one thing you could change about your past, what would it be?"

What was I doing?

Finn's wide eyes asked the same question.

The air felt charged as everyone waited for the answer. He'd done so much, he'd hurt so many, including every one of us. How would he respond?

After what felt like ten minutes, Geoffrey's voice seemed to come from nowhere. "Nothing. I'd change nothing."

"Seriously?" Pyra demanded. I braced a hand on her thigh, though she didn't seem like she was about to pop up and attack him. "Seriously? Nothing?"

"Nothing. Every action I took created the person I am today." His voice was quiet, almost reedy. I got the sense he was pulling from deep down. "I made many mistakes. I trusted a lot of the wrong people, but I learned something from every one of those actions. Now I'm better for it—in this moment."

Those must have been the magic words, because none of us could come up with a single thing to say in response. Instead, we curled up, finding heat where we could, and rested our heads on our pillows. I was out before I could give his words any more thought.

Chapter 20

We pushed hard for two days, driving deeper into the mountains, fighting fey without hesitation, a desperate urge to move faster, to strike harder, driving every step, every thrust of our weapons, every strained chew of our food.

We were all stressed to our limits and soaked in blood, but we'd remained hopeful. Especially the night before Geoffrey finally told us we would arrive at the labyrinth. A sense of anticipation draped around us as we rolled out sleeping bags and hastily washed our exposed skin in the frozen chill of a nearby brook. It clung to me like fresh spiderwebs as we dozed off.

"Up and att'em." The shout in my ear sent a shockwave through my slumbering body.

I shot upright up in bed, squinting in the near darkness, an array of colorful magics clutched in my fist. My half-asleep mind cranked furiously, trying to figure out which attack would work the fastest... when I realized it was the Fire God beaming at me as she dangled one of Lachlan's signature granola bars before my face.

I slumped over again, my forehead dropping to my open palms. "I hate you so much."

"You can't hate me." Pyra rolled a sucker between her teeth. "I'm far too loveable. Like a panda bear. Do you know anyone who hates panda bears?"

"Pandas have zero reason for their continued existence," Lachlan groused. He, too, sat upright in his bedroll across our small circle, scrubbing wearily at his bloodshot eyes. "I don't know if that means I hate them, though."

Pyra thrust her candy in the air triumphantly. "Exactly. Un-hate-able. Now stand up and help me get everyone else on their feet. We don't have a ton of time to work with if we want to reach the labyrinth in time."

With a sigh, I shoved my blankets off. "Is it morning?" I peered up through the trees, unable to see much through the foliage. "This feels like three. The sun isn't up."

"It's definitely not three in the morning," Finn called, covering up a yawn. Joseph helped him to his feet. "It's before six. Maybe about five minutes before."

The kelpie was the only one of us, aside from Geoffrey, who bothered to wear a watch. I'd left my phone on the plane because it was more of an annoyance than anything, and the soldiers who'd brought theirs had grumbled on the second day when the tech suddenly went dead.

"If *someone* would pull her weight around here, you'd be able to see that yourself." Pyra shot me a pointed glance.

Oh. Right. Per my usual morning habit, I reached out and, with some serious effort, forced the thickest black clouds to disperse. Murky, gray sunshine spilled through the thick sheet of clouds that remained, revealing it was, in fact, daytime.

I felt drained all the time now—and not just from the hiking. The weather had gotten worse the deeper we wandered into the mountain range. I fended off the worst of the rainstorms that choked the forests, but the near-constant drizzle was beyond my reach.

Saran wrap crinkled as I unwrapped the granola bar and shoved it in my mouth. I chewed methodically, knowing I needed to eat to keep up my strength. But, stars, would I be glad to never see a granola bar

169

in my life ever again.

As I checked my things, taking care to ensure the forbidden dagger remained tucked deep in the bottom of my bag, I nudged Ryder with my elbow.

"Time to get up," I murmured. It wasn't like him to stay in bed like this. Normally, he was the one helping everyone get sorted out. Yet, even the laziest of the soldiers was on his feet across the camp and Ryder had yet to rouse. "A little farther and then you can sleep all you want."

I shoved the last of the food in my mouth and turned my attention on my bedroll. A few grumbles and some ungainly punches, and I finally twisted it into a haphazard ball that would fit into my bag. Satisfied with the result, I rocked back on my heels and glanced back to see what Ryder thought of my mess. A tingle ran down my spine when I found him still laying there, prone.

He hadn't woken up with a sarcastic comment about the conditions. He hadn't plucked at my increasingly ratty braid. No, he lay there, barely moving. My gut twisted. Hard. The granola bar congealed into a lump.

Don't panic, I told myself, approaching him slowly. "Hey, Ryder? You ok?"

No response.

He'd never left me waiting like this before. I didn't think he was capable.

My heart thundered in my chest. My skin felt clammy in a way that had nothing to do with the fine mist that coated it like dew. I knelt beside the incubus and touched his face tentatively. The stubble on his chin prickled my palm, but beneath it, his skin felt chilled. He mumbled under his breath, cheek turning into my hand, but his beautiful eyes remained closed. I leaned farther over him, close enough the ragged ends of my hair caught on the grass around his head.

"Ryder?" My voice rang louder than I'd intended, hysteria thrashing inside me like the sea in a thunderstorm. It drew the attention of the rest of our group. Leaves crunched and Oron crouched on Ryder's other side, palms up on his knees.

"What's wrong with him?" Pyra asked for the both of them. "Why won't he wake up?"

I ran my hand down his chest. He felt so cold. I forced the words past the sticky lump in my throat. "I don't know." To the incubus, I said, "Ryder, if you can hear me, open your eyes, nod your head. Anything. Come on, talk to me."

More errant mumbling, but otherwise nothing changed. Deep lines of stress fanned out from the corners of his eyes and crisscrossed the bridge of his nose. He shivered despite the heat Pyra and I poured over him.

But he wouldn't wake.

My fingers dug into his shirt as I leaned farther over him, fear snapping sharply like a snare drum in my ears. He wasn't sick. I would be able to see that with my abilities. He wasn't dehydrated, and he'd seemed ok last night before bed. I wondered if it had been something he'd eaten or drank.

I called his name again.

"We need to get moving."

I may have mostly forgiven Geoffrey for all the crap he'd done to me and my friends, but there were times, like now, where I truly resented him. His boots moved into my periphery near the crown of Ryder's head, and my teeth ground together.

"Zara, we're almost there," he said. "The labyrinth is through the tree line, close to here. It will take us about two hours to get through the maze, and then we're at the caverns. But we need to get moving. Now."

"Slow your roll, man." Pyra leaped to her feet and shoved him. "He's sick. Let her figure out what's going on and deal with it."

Oron stared at me for another minute. Something about his presence seemed more intense than normal, before he shoved to his feet and joined Pyra somewhere to my left. I heard some scuffling, like someone being shoved, but I shifted my attention back to the incubus.

I peeled back his eyelid, frowning at his non-reactive pupils. The throb of the pulse in his neck beneath my fingers remained steady. Slow but steady.

"Please," I pleaded. "If you can hear me, wake up. I don't know what to do."

"You don't understand," Geoffrey snapped somewhere over my head. "If we don't enter the maze within the next thirty minutes, we'll have to wait another twenty-four hours. I don't know the patterns if we leave much later, and I won't be able to guide us through. And we definitely, definitely don't want to get trapped in there after dark—assuming the walls don't crush us first."

Another person dropped beside me. I tensed before I recognized the many bracelets wrapped around Finn's wrists. He pressed his hand against Ryder's chest, and I looked up at him. The worry in his emerald gaze reflected the turmoil I felt twisting my insides, swirling and slashing like a blender on steroids.

"He's critically low on energy," Finn whispered so only I could hear. "It's extremely rare for daemoni to get this low in their energy pool, but he is." He rocked back on his heels and chewed lightly on his lip ring, considering. "I don't know why he didn't feed before we left. He knew we were heading out here, but he refused to go…"

A faint hum filled my ears, and I smoothed Ryder's brow, wishing I could erase the worry lines festering there. No. Not worry lines. Stress lines. He hadn't fed. I knew it was because of me. I remembered how angry I'd gotten when he'd snuck back to the hostel after a night of feeding on errant energy. He probably hadn't wanted to upset me again, but we weren't exactly physically close these days…

And I'd monopolized his evenings and nights, needing him to stay with me while I slept. He had gone nowhere, choosing to stay by my side and forfeit his own needs. I pressed my hand to my mouth and sucked in a sharp gasp, trying to think straight.

Finn frowned when I drew back. "Z?"

I barely heard the kelpie, too caught up in my thoughts. I loathed how still Ryder was beneath my hands, his lack of response to my questions. I needed him here with me. Not wanted. Needed. And now that I couldn't get him to respond... I needed to help him. He'd helped me so many times before. Now it was my turn to return the favor.

And I knew what I needed to do.

"Zara, I know how much you care for the incubus, but waiting for him puts everyone at risk." Geoffrey knelt beside me and I ducked my head. "We need to leave him behind and go *now*."

Finn held up an arm. "She—"

Pyra broke in, "Maybe Finn can stay with him, make sure he's safe until we get back."

"We aren't leaving him behind." My words were a snap of bitter wind on the darkest of nights. I straightened, keeping my thigh firmly pressed against Ryder's side, letting him know I was with him in his vulnerable state. I glared at Geoffrey. "Everyone needs to back off and give me a minute to freaking *think*. If I don't—"

I would crack.

I would break.

I would burn.

I didn't finish the sentence, but Pyra understood. She knew how close to the edge I was, how my toes peeked over the precipice. She nodded once and threw out her arms, flames fanning her leathers like wings, forcing everyone but Finn, who remained glued to my side, back.

"You heard the lady; she needs a minute. Now back up before I make you—yes, that includes you, Leon." A few soldiers grumbled, but their voices faded as Pyra berated them into acquiescence. "Let's go check out this entrance so we're prepared when Zara and Ryder are ready to go."

Finn squeezed my shoulder. "I know what you're thinking, but this will be ok. I've known Ryder an incredibly long time, and while I haven't been with you guys much over the past month, I know he wouldn't want to pressure you into anything. Don't feel like you have to—"

"That's great and all, Finn, but this is partially my fault," I said. "I should have opened up more to him about how I was feeling. We should have had more conversations about our issues. But I didn't, and now here we are." I swiped the back of my hand over my nose. "He knew seeing him feed upset me though I had no right to be upset. I barely let him sit near me after Ridley died. I couldn't stand looking at him for weeks. I knew how I felt about him, how much I liked him, but I wasn't ready to commit to anything. And I—"

"It's ok to be conflicted." Finn ignored the angry shove of my arm and pulled me against his side. "Your relationship may be complicated, but it isn't any more complicated than most relationships. We all go through trials; we all battle through problems. Some of us make it, some of us don't. But you guys were pushing through."

I turned my skin to ice, not wanting to hear this, not sure I was prepared to hear the words that were sure to follow. But Finn wouldn't relent.

"Hey, enough of that. Look at me." He waited for me to shove my hair aside and meet his eyes. "Zara, you're not any less of the woman you've always been—and he's still the same arrogant, dark horse prince I've always known. You might not be one hundred percent on where you stand with him, but I've *seen* you two together. I've *watched* how you interact. There's something that runs between you two that delves far deeper than any stupid fated bond—broken or not."

Finn's lips pressed into a white line as he thought over his next words. "You two have always burned hot, so much so it freaked me out at first. I told Ryder to keep his distance because I didn't want him sweeping you up in some romance you weren't ready for. But Zara—some of that flash and bang has faded, but the heat hasn't. And you're finally letting it breathe. And I'm glad to see that… but you need to know that whatever you decide here, it isn't end-all, be-all."

My heart skipped in my chest, his words sinking into my skin like rain in the desert.

"He made his choices, and if I know him half as well as I do, he is fine with those choices." Finn smoothed my braid. "And he wouldn't want you acting rashly, doing something you might not be ready for. I know we're crunched for time, but I will stay behind and watch over him, keep him safe, so you can go on ahead. We'll wait for you guys to return to the entrance of the labyrinth."

Grass swayed beside my knees in the subtle breeze. Somewhere in the distance the rest of our group chattered, but I focused on the rustle of the dry blades, the chill of the misty air.

"He worries about my soul." My words spilled from me, broken and jagged. "That with the bond broken, he'll steal bits and pieces of it. That we can't be together because of—"

"Z, you're a God. The first God to ever possess more than one element. The only person I've ever known to beat death not once, not twice, not three times." Finn pulled me against him in a tight hug I hadn't known I'd missed until now. I inhaled his wintermint scent, appreciating him for all that he meant to me right now.

Finn continued, "I highly doubt Ryder could steal the tiniest bit of your soul, even if he tried."

Finn was right.

He had to be right.

Ryder and I had been through so much already. For something as trivial as that to hold us back—it was simply inconceivable. I nodded against Finn's chest and peeled away. He squinted, taking in my expression, and smiled, releasing me.

I bent over the incubus again, feeling him breathe beneath my hand. He'd always been so beautiful to me, darkly handsome in a way I never quite believed. From the moment his golden eyes had locked with mine back in that club, I'd felt it. The click. A subtle shift that had nothing to do with the krav legara bond, and everything to do with attraction. I traced the high sweep of his cheekbone, the point in his cheek where I knew his single dimple would appear.

But it was more than that, more than his innate beauty and the draw of his magic. It was the way he'd allowed me space when I demanded it, how he'd made me laugh when I felt like crying, how he hadn't blamed me for his brother's death, how he continued to root for us, though it felt like the odds were stacked against us.

"I'm not leaving him behind."

"Then you know what you have to do." Finn stood. "I'll give you two a minute."

I swallowed hard, suddenly shy for no good reason, and slipped my fingers into Ryder's hair. My face lowered until it lined up with his, eyes to eyes, nose to nose... lips to lips. I hovered there, a mere half-inch separating our skin, and I rubbed his cheek again, his stubble catching on my callouses.

"Ryder, you've told me before that you're ready when I am. And if you can hear me... I'm ready."

And then I closed the gap, my lips brushing his once, twice, three times.

It felt strange, being the one to initiate this kiss despite knowing exactly how he felt about me, remembering the words he'd pledged to me. Part of me wondered if it wasn't already too late.

I leaned farther into him, felt the stutter-step of his heartbeat as it quickened beneath my hands. His lips twitched beneath mine. Subtle, but definitely there. Encouraged, I kissed him again, my fingers weaving into his thick hair, magic lacing my lips, a silent promise. I knew what I was offering him, knew I was finally ready for him.

I hoped he would accept it.

Accept me.

For one dangerously long moment, he didn't answer, his lips falling still beneath mine. For one horribly long moment, I screwed up my eyes, wondering if I'd been too late, if I'd waited too long, if I'd—

His arms came up around me, one pinning me to his chest and the other drawing my head closer to his, smashing our lips together hungrily, needily. He devoured me like I was his favorite treat, and when a growl rumbled in his throat, I didn't hold back my smile, feeling it radiate through me like sunshine.

This was right.

We were right.

And we were exactly where we needed to be.

My head tilted to the side, seeking a better angle, and I parted my lips. I felt him hesitate, opened my eyes, and found his warm amber ones fixed on me, soft and hazy with want. When he accepted the magic I offered freely, I gasped. Pleasure rippled through me as he sipped on my magic, drawing it up through me...

And he broke away, turning his head to the side at the last moment, before the power slipped down his throat, breaking our kiss. He still clutched me close, holding me steady in his lap. My heart hammered so hard I felt him vibrating with the rhythm. Or maybe it was the other way around. I couldn't tell anymore. The sound of our panting filled the air as I waited desperately for him to speak, needed to know what words were going to spill from his mouth first.

He gulped, his fingers massaging the back of my head, our foreheads pressed flat together. My eyelashes brushed his, we were crushed so close together. His golden eyes swirled as they met mine. "I'm not taking this from you. Not unless—"

I pressed a finger to his mouth, silencing him. "I already told you: I'm ready for this. I'm ready for you. It took me long enough, but I'm one-hundred percent here, with you, right now."

I don't know who moved first, only that our lips crashed together, our hands tugging at our clothes, trying to pull the other closer than was physically possible, as if trying to inhabit the other's skin and become one.

Golden arcs of my magic spilled from me, filling him, electrifying his eyes, warming his skin. When he finally drank his fill, our kisses grew less frantic, our desperate hands and exploring fingers less eager, and we sank into one another, enjoying the feeling of just... being together.

After a few minutes of lying there, in Ryder's arms, loving the feel of him around me, I leaned back and brushed some hair from his forehead, suddenly shy. His thumb smoothed across my lips, his eyes glued to mine. I'd never seen the color in them so rich or molten before.

"You're back." I lightly pecked his chin.

"So I am," he whispered. "And your soul is still yours."

"So it is."

He tightened his grip around my middle. "All that worry for nothing."

"Maybe not for nothing."

He tapped my nose, then sat up with a grunt, careful to not jostle me too much. "You and me, glowstick, we still have a lot to discuss."

"When we're back home, we can spend all day talking. Maybe all week." I clambered to my feet, but still held Ryder's hand, not wanting to fully break from him yet.

"I'm holding you to that."

Chapter 21

I t was just a short, even path bracketed by sandy-colored stone. A short path littered with tiny chunks of white rock that maybe looked like little pieces of bone, crushed by the fifteen-story-high walls that ran parallel to one another. A short path that connected with a bunch of longer, twistier paths through which we may or may not escape.

"If we don't turn back now, we are the most stupid people alive," Joseph murmured in front of me. It shocked me, hearing him say that. He was normally the voice of perseverance, mind over mission. The fact that he was rattled by what awaited us in the labyrinth before us had the bizarre effect of calming me down.

An arm brushed my shoulder and Lachlan grinned wildly, eyes fixed on the entrance to the maze that would likely chew us up and spit us out—literally. He popped his knuckles in quick succession. "This is the best day ever."

We found ourselves in the heart of the mountain range, standing at the base of two, possibly three peaks; Geoffrey had indicated this maze wound around at least one of them. Thick, nearly purple clouds hung low, grazing the tops of the maze's walls. The mist occasionally dipped down, the soft and subtle touch like fingers brushing on our skin. I loathed it, but I couldn't expend any more energy on the weather. I needed to save it for what stood ahead.

179

"Speed and stealth are your best friends in there," Geoffrey yelled. He moved to the front of our group, right on the outside of the opening to the maze. I swore something big sighed from within its depths. "You move when and how I move. You stop when I stop. And no matter what, you stay absolutely silent once we cross inside. If you can't do that, we can't hear what will happen next, and that is a very. Big. Problem." His bicolored gaze would have cleaved us in two if it were a weapon. "Any questions while you can still ask them?"

An ant crawling across the ground made more sound than us.

I'd known Geoffrey as a leader, had spoken to him as an equal, but I'd never heard him quite so commanding before. "Very good. Now let's go before the pattern changes."

Lach jumped in front of me with Pyra, his eagerness to get inside apparent. Ryder took my back, with Finn, Joseph, and Oron lagging behind. The rest of the soldiers followed our lead, most with their thumbs hooked on the straps of their bags, eyes wide as they entered the labyrinth, struggling to keep their movements as silent as possible.

Once inside the massive walls marking the belly of the beast, all outside noise dropped away. I'd thought the woods had been silent. I'd been wrong. In here, I imagined I could hear my sweat pooling in my pores; each tiny gasp or misplaced step ricocheted like gunfire in an alley.

It wasn't until we'd hung our first left, leaving the forest behind us, that I heard the first rumble of stone against stone. It sent shudders crawling down my skin, like hearing a mountain lion growling as it hovered above on a tall rock. It got worse when Geoffrey motioned us right, his head cocked to the side as he listened intently.

Something big and heavy crashed together and Geoffrey took off, sprinting full-speed down the straightaway. Half a beat later, Lachlan was on his heels, with the rest of us popping from six to sixty in no time flat. The gnashing, crashing tumble of rock against rock roared.

Halfway down, I risked a glance behind us. The limestone walls folded together, accordion-like in their movement, bowing inward, nipping at the heels of the last Earth soldier in line.

Ryder snagged my elbow, nearly yanking my shoulder from its socket as he ripped me sideways, as I saw the man vanish between the folds of the rock—one arm reaching for his nearest companion. He hadn't had time to scream as the stone closed around him. My stomach clenched tight, my nerves on fire.

We stopped almost as suddenly, nerves shot, barely breathing as adrenaline fired hot, dragging people into the passageway as quickly as we could. Not four seconds later, the passage closed with a violent snap. Where there had been a T intersection was now a dead-end.

I understood now what Geoffrey meant by the necessity for silence.

He motioned forward with a slash of his arm, and we continued. We didn't have a choice in the matter. It was forward... or death.

As we pushed deeper into the maze, the grumbling of stone grated on my already shot nerves. Sometimes it sounded up ahead, other times it rumbled from behind—a beast trailing our frightened rabbit footsteps. The maze seemed to follow no rhyme or reason. I couldn't predict its pattern.

To survive, I put my utmost faith in Geoffrey, since he seemed to possess an uncanny connection with the labyrinth. He understood the markings on the walls, the rumblings of the rock, far better than any of the rest of us. It led to some strange patterns. Sometimes he would stop and slam his back against the wall and wait for several agonizing minutes, and other times he shouted for us to speed up, running faster than we'd ever thought possible.

Several times I tripped when I shot from practically standing still to sprinting. Many of us did. Nearly all of us got back up again, no matter our scraped palms or aching knees. Exhaustion pulled at our limbs, stank in our sweat, but time and time again, we shrugged it off, forcing ourselves to stay alert, ready.

Hours later, it was impossible to tell how many, I swiped dirt from my forehead, gasping from our latest eighty-foot sprint, wondering when it would stop, wondering how far we'd come. Ryder nudged my shoulder, his eyes asking me the questions his mouth couldn't. I shook my head. I would be fine.

Up ahead, Geoffrey signaled left and tore off to the side. Shards of blue-gray gravel flew beneath my shoes as I rocketed down a narrow crevice, ears straining to hear the telltale rumble of the beast smudging out our progress. This time, it didn't come. But, as I was learning, the waiting was sometimes worse. It led to wondering, limbs locked tight, head drawn down beneath hunched shoulders, a hive of bees buzzing in my belly, wondering if we'd made a wrong turn.

If everything was about to end.

It was one thing being stalked; it was an entirely different thing *knowing* you were prey. It had been a long time since I'd last been prey. Funny how that had involved Geoffrey, too.

I barely had time to think beyond basic instinct as we wove deeper into the mountain pass, the stress winding my muscles tight, the neurons in my brain firing at full capacity. I'd abandoned thoughts of magic ages ago, glad I'd stopped holding back the skies from the start. I wouldn't have been able to maintain my focus that long, anyway. And it wasn't like we needed my protection. No matter how damp our hair, skin and clothing got, the ground remained remarkably dry and dusty.

Even Kaleal was juiced, riding low right behind my eyes, staying silent while her sharp gaze missed nothing. I got the feeling she didn't want to distract me, didn't want anything to go wrong.

Impossibly, Geoffrey ran faster ahead of us, and without complaint, we all complied with his unspoken command. My thigh muscles burned, but I pushed harder, eyes fixed on the dark vee of sweat that ran down Finn's back.

Comply or die.

Chapter 22

"We're here," Geoffrey said. They were the first words any of us had heard in far too long.

"Thank the stars," someone shouted. Others quickly joined in a chorus of relieved voices.

I agreed, but I didn't have enough air left in my lungs to vocalize that fact. I'd never been more grateful to hear two words in my life.

I collapsed against the wall of the canyon, chest heaving, hands ground against a pair of brutal stitches in my sides, uncaring of the rough rock digging into my back. My legs had gone numb a while back, but now that we'd stopped, fire scored through them. My lungs screamed, demanding more oxygen, faster than humanly possible.

"Never again." Finn dropped to the ground, arms wrapped around his middle, gagging. "I don't care how bored I get in the office. Never again will I dream about how much more exciting my life would be if it had more adventure in it."

"I second that," said Joseph. He tossed his bag on the ground at Finn's feet with a groan and lowered himself beside the kelpie, arms hooked behind his head, shirt practically black with sweat. He leaned his head against the rock wall, face horizontal with the sky, and swiped some of his hair out of his eyes. "I can't believe we did that. And survived."

My legs shook like a newborn colt's, and I dropped before they collapsed, slumped over across from the couple. Joseph definitely had the right idea. I shrugged off my pack with a groan of relief. I set it next to my knee, beside Joseph's.

Having finally cooled some of the inferno threatening to burn my blood, I offered a weak smile. "Oh, come on now, outrunning an enemy you couldn't see or predict? That was fun."

Joseph stared at me like I'd grown a third arm or sprouted tusks. Finn coiled, leaned forward, and rapped my forehead with two bony knuckles. "There is something extremely wrong with you."

Lachlan bent in two, stretching his calf muscles, then hopped up and down a few times, pumping his arms at his side. He was barely winded, smiling like an absolute weirdo. "Now that's what I call a warm-up."

"Remind me to punch you when I rise from the dead." Ryder mopped at his face with the lower half of his shirt. I would have salivated over his cut muscles if I'd had any moisture whatsoever left within me.

"If anyone deserves a good haunting, it's you," he continued.

Lach bent his arm to examine a shallow cut on his elbow. "Don't be jelly. I'm just that awesome."

"As if I'd ever be jealous of you."

When my breathing finally evened out and I didn't feel like I'd puke all over my shoes, I used the wall at my back to lever myself upright, searching intently for water. We'd stopped in a circular area with five passageways splintering off in different directions. The paths were so narrow I wasn't sure I would fit through them, even squeezing sideways.

Pyra leaned against the entrance to one, toying with a cigarette. She held it up, squinted at it, then lifted a purple lollipop in the other. With a resigned sigh, she shoved the candy between her lips and tucked the cigarette back into one of her many vest pockets.

Oron stood near Geoffrey in the center of the circle, hand loosely gripping his scimitar, gazing up at the craggy cliffs of a mountain peak that nearly covered the murky sun. An open bag at his feet revealed the caps of several plastic water bottles. Geoffrey's lips were moving, his finger jumping in a pattern over the passageways, as if reciting a chant that would guide his next decision.

I snatched up my bag and, bones creaking, body protesting, slouched over to join them. After downing nearly a full bottle of water, I asked, "Where are we?"

"Here," Oron signed cheekily.

I cuffed his arm. "How are you holding up?"

"Never better." His hands stilled, then moved again, elegant as any ballet dancer. "I used to run up the pyramid stairs before breakfast every morning. Definitely more predictable, though a lot less interesting. I'm ready to…" He gave a little jerk, face turning toward me, fist firming around the handle of his weapon. His bicep bulged, and he released the blade with effort. "I'm eager to get this over with."

I frowned. Something about that statement struck me a little wrong.

"That's the passage," Geoffrey said. He pointed at the narrowest opening. Internally, I groaned. "We won't be able to fit many people through. There isn't a ton of space to work with anyway, but that's where we'll find the cave where I hid the weapons."

This close to the end, the weight of my bag dangling from my hand felt immense. I squeezed the strap.

Pyra raised a hand and flapped it around. "What about Oron? Couldn't he, I don't know, widen the space?"

Oron shook his head when Geoffrey motioned toward him. His fingers flew. "The earth isn't normal here, like it's more human than stone. I can barely manipulate what's beneath our feet let alone the walls."

I rubbed my face. My sweat had dried, leaving a crusty residue. I, too, had noticed my control over the Air felt *less* somehow, as if whatever spell restricted flight also limited use of the element entirely. The Order truly had outdone itself with this obnoxious obstacle course.

"How many people are we talking here?" Ryder asked.

Geoffrey scanned our faces. "We'll keep it to Joseph and Zara." He scoffed at Joseph's affronted scoff. "Like I trust you to not kill me the earliest chance you have."

"If they go, I go," Oron signed. "I want to be the only one handling that sling."

Pyra piped up, "Like sin if you think I'm staying behind. I escaped death so I could see this hoard of yours. Not to avoid it."

Geoffrey closed his eyes. "Fine. The Gods may go. But no one else."

Thunderclouds rolled across Ryder's face. I braced a hand on his forearm before he could argue. "That's fine. We can each grab our weapon, then get out of there. No need for a bunch of extra people blocking the way. Wait—" I looked to Geoffrey— "These passages. They don't close?"

He scratched his head through his hair. "We're safe in this circle and in the passages that lead to the caverns. The paths do continue onward in a few different directions from there. We'll want to avoid those however possible."

I nodded. This maze reminded me of a spiderweb. Spiders navigated their self-inflicted puzzle by skittering along non-sticky strands of silk. Geoffrey employed similar techniques, whether or not he realized it.

Ryder lifted my arm and held it, drawing me close as his thumb swirled in circles on the underside of my wrist. I shivered. "Are you sure you're ok with this? I know Pyra will be there, but the other three…"

"I'll be fine." I lifted a ball of water, evaporated it, then hefted a bundle of flames. "I'm still me, remember? As kickass as always. I'll be in and out of that cavern so quick you won't have time to miss me."

"I know." He turned me so my back was to him. His fingers dug into my gnarled braid, and I felt him unraveling it, picking out the sticks and mud amid the sweaty strands. "And I know it's probably me, but

187

something about this doesn't feel right, like I've missed a very obvious clue."

His fingers stilled before resuming their methodical motions, smoothing my hair and plucking out the knots. "It's not that I don't want you out of my sight, or that I don't trust you to handle yourself, but I don't want anything to happen to you somewhere that I can't help you."

I closed my eyes as he began a familiar process of binding up my hair, twisting and turning it in a pattern I recognized, embraced. "I know, but I promise, it will be ok. We didn't come this far only for it all to fall apart now."

He wrapped the tiny black hairband around the tail of his masterpiece and pressed his lips to the top of my head, hand cupping the image of his sigil he'd woven in my locks. It was a sigil I'd avoided since he and Ridley fought over me back at the mansion after I'd finally found out what it meant to him—like a girl wearing a letterman's jacket in high school.

"You're right." Ryder pressed a cool kiss to my forehead. I pulled back, squinting into his face, lightly touching his jaw. He didn't look as convinced as he sounded. "Keep your senses sharp, alright?"

"Yo, lovebirds, you're making me sick." Pyra clapped my back. "In case you forgot, we've got a life-or-death mission to complete."

I squeezed the incubus tight, a thought occurring to me. "Hey, would you watch my stuff?" I nudged my bag over with my toe. "I don't want to bring it with me. It's going to be a squeeze as it is."

Ryder hefted the bag and slung it over this shoulder. "No problem. Now get going."

Thank the stars. Relief rolled over me, crashed through me. I still didn't believe a word of what Kaleal said to be true, but it felt better to err on the side of caution. If Joseph got the chakram, he could use it to create the bonds of peace, and then this whole nightmare would be over.

I jogged to catch up with Pyra at the entrance of the passage.

At her side, Joseph hefted his pack and patted it. "I've got my half of the chakram right here. We get in there, we see if the two pieces fit together, and we make this thing happen. If it doesn't work, we get out of there and get it back to HQ as quick as we can." He lifted a single brow. "Anyone have any issues with that?"

Nope. I shook my head. The sooner we did this, the sooner I would be able to breathe again.

Geoffrey glanced up at the sky as if evaluating the angle of the sun. His cheek twitched, and he shared an expression rife with secrets with me, then faced the passage. He gripped two rocks and hefted himself up with a grunt.

"Stick close," he said.

It was a tight squeeze, one that forced us to contort and twist in unpleasant ways. Hands scrambled over stones and feet caught in divots, our strenuous efforts occasionally punctuated by cursing as we pushed forward. I carefully monitored Oron's motions, mirroring his hand- and foot-holds, while wondering what he had meant before and why it still bothered me.

A few minutes more and the passage opened up into a pregnant bulge in the side of the mountain. I scrubbed the cuts on my hands, frowning. The Hand tugged on his collar and scanned the rock face of the mountain as we situated ourselves in a semicircle around him. For once, Joseph stood close to me, and I felt like a bridge had fallen over the long divide between us.

Geoffrey grunted, twisted something, and stone scraped across stone. Out of habit, I glanced toward the trail where it continued farther away from the mountain, splitting off in several directions. When the passage didn't get gobbled up, I turned to Geoffrey who grinned, arm spread wide as he ushered us into a hole cut in the side of the mountain.

"You make this look easy," Pyra grumbled. She took care to not touch the Hand as she walked past him, flames roaring in her gloved palms. "Are you sure we needed you for this?"

"And you would have discovered this cavern... how?" Geoffrey asked lightly. "These caves can only be opened by me, too. I think it has something to do with the brands and my connection to all of you."

"But you don't have magic anymore," Joseph observed, then growled when he crashed into my back. "Zara, you can't stop in the middle of the door—oh, wow."

Wow didn't begin to cover how I felt. Geoffrey had vastly undersold the spectacular trove tucked away in these mountains. I twined my fingers around the vial at my neck, the chain biting into my skin. I'd thought Phenex's vault of gems and gold was rich, but this put his stash to shame. From quartz statues aligned six wide and twelve deep in one corner to piles of paintings stacked against the opposite wall—and the mountain of gemstones on pedestals that flickered in the torches Pyra had lit... I didn't know where to focus first.

"This is a van Gogh." Wooden frames clacked as Pyra flipped through a stack of paintings. "Picasso, Monet, Rembrandt, Hokusai, Yoshida—" She hefted a canvass over her head and waved it back and forth, jaw slack. "Banksy? What are these doing here?"

"It's not only the paintings." Joseph gingerly hefted a vase, checked the base, and shook his head. "Some of these I recognize, most I don't. But the signatures... they seem legit. I can't believe the Order has hidden this all away."

"Is it difficult to believe?" Geoffrey joined me as I gazed up into the face of a statue featuring a woman with a beak instead of a nose and twisting snakes for hair. Balt spots intermixed among the feathers decorating her arms, as if she'd been recently plucked. "Since the fall of the Originals, the Order has gotten everything it wanted."

A low whistle drew my attention to the center of the room where

190

Oron ignored the spill of golden coins at his feet as he crouched before an object shaped like a Y. He touched two grooves notched in the uplifted arms. He turned to us. "Davarius's sling," he signed one-handed.

The cord and cradle were back in Rome.

Pyra whooped, abandoning her paintings, and snagged a broadsword braced against the wall—at least, I assumed it was a sword since it lacked a cross guard. She hefted it over her head, angling the metal so it gleamed in the firelight. "It's lighter than I thought it would be."

Ash always was a clever one, Kaleal murmured, emerging for the first time since we'd entered the forest. *He loved these weapons like they were his children.*

I swallowed hard and approached the trident leaning on the opposite wall. It stood taller than I did. I gripped the staff, found it fit my hands easily. A pair of spikes set in a U shape topped it. I lowered the points. Pyra was right. I'd expected it to feel heavier. The metal shimmered blue, and its prongs were maybe a foot long, topped with ninety-degree points—a shape and style I was very familiar with. Between them, in the middle, was a hole where my dagger would go.

"Hey guys, come over here." In the center of the room, Joseph stood beside a marble pedestal. Propped on top was a half-circle of metal shaped like a D. The curved side of it was propped up in some sort of clever device that held it upright. Joseph reached for the flat side of the weapon and hefted it, bouncing it up and down, getting a feel for its weight. I realized then the chakram was both designed to be thrown as one full circle and split apart to serve as two separate blades.

Fascinating.

Did you not hear me before? Kaleal griped. *Ash would be thrilled to see these put to use again.*

Joseph gently set the curve of metal back on the stand. He turned to us, eyes bright and wicked with hope. It lit a spark inside me, one that had come dangerously close to blowing out. "This is it. If the pieces fit, we could put an end to the war. Our problems… they'll be solved."

He made a point of looking right at me when he said it. I allowed his words to reverberate through me, hopeful for more than just the end of the world's biggest crisis yet.

"Well, get on with it." Pyra jumped up and down, hair flying around her face. "Get out the other half. Let's see if they'll fit."

"Yeah, sure." Joseph sounded dazed. He crouched beside his bag and tugged on the ties keeping it shut. He shoved his hand inside and felt around, his smile diminishing and his brow creasing. "What the—"

A wadded-up ball of fabric rolled out of the top, followed by some clothing. A ball of fabric I, myself, had pounded into shape this morning. My pulse thudded, low and slow, gaining speed, a dawning sense of horror shooting through me. My skin prickled as I realized—

"I don't think—" Joseph overturned the bag, its guts spilling across the carpet of gold coins like discarded trash. He snagged a granola bar off the ground and groaned. "Zara, this is your stuff. You must have grabbed my bag by accident earlier."

I barely heard him through the whooshing in my ears. I was shaking, shaking so hard my teeth practically clattered in my head. Pyra slapped her hand across her mouth, catching sight of what had captured my attention. Oron lifted his head, and I felt his glare pinning me in place.

No. No, no, no.

This could not be happening right now.

Joseph scowled, "What are you—" He turned back to the items and went still. There, amid the diamonds and emeralds, looking like it belonged perfectly, lay a dagger of rippling blue steel. It had come free from the cloth Lachlan had wrapped it in when he'd stolen it back from the Order.

Geoffrey looked from the dagger to me, to the trident that I clung to as the only thing holding me upright. He opened his mouth, then closed it, his fingers finding the oaths burned across his forehead.

This was so incredibly bad.

Joseph coughed out a single laugh. One chock full of disbelief and disdain. It shattered me.

"I can't believe this. I can't believe this is happening right now." He paused, then lashed out. We flinched as coins launched across the room, clattering off bits of armor and embedding themselves into the wall. He stared up at me, his expression hauntingly dead. "No, actually. I can believe it. Because you couldn't resist, could you, Zara? You had to make this about you somehow—"

I reached for him, to do what, I didn't know. I just knew I had to fix this. Somehow. "No, that's not—"

He knocked away my hand. "You had to say you'd do one thing." He snatched up the dagger and stood, brandishing it at me. I stumbled backward, the trident clattering to the ground as I retreated. "And, naturally, you went and did another. You said you were with us on this one, Zara." Joseph was practically shouting. "You said you wanted to fix everything. And you know what... you had me."

He laughed again, that ugly, awful sound ripped straight from his chest. "I turned my back on every single of my doubts about you, and I went with you on this one. Then you go and pull this on us." Joseph stopped advancing on me. He dragged his hand across his open mouth, staring somewhere over my shoulder. "But not anymore. I'm going to fix this once and for all."

"What are you going to do?" I lunged for him, snagged his sleeve. He threw his elbow back, catching me in the jaw, and I fell back. Desperation curdled like spoiled milk in my gut. My eyes flashed from him to the dagger and back. "What are you going to do?"

"I'm solving the problem." He stomped toward the exit. "First, I'm finding the chakram and I'm going to put an end to this whole nuclear nightmare." He turned back around, the sunlight at his back glinting across the dagger as he thrust it overhead. "And second, I'm getting rid of this. Or securing it. I don't care right now. Whatever it takes to make sure you don't get it back."

He whipped around, wind howling around him as he finally pulled himself together again. But before he fully left the chamber, he turned and looked straight at me over his shoulder. "And Zara, when this crisis is over, there's no need for you to ever visit headquarters again."

I dropped to my knees, anguish ripping through me.

How had everything gone so wrong?

Oron darted past me, rushing after Joseph, likely to make sure he didn't do something too incredibly impulsive. Pyra and Geoffrey lingered. I felt their stares melting into my back, ut I couldn't lift my head, couldn't look at them. I didn't know what to say and knew no matter what the explanation was… it wasn't enough.

Two minutes passed. Three. Four. The silence clung to me like saran wrap.

It was Pyra who broke the silence. "This is totally fucked."

"I'll say," Geoffrey agreed. He sighed, and a hand dropped into my line of vision. "Come on, get up."

I stared at the limb as if I'd never seen one before. "I messed up," I whispered.

"Yeah." Pyra kicked at some coins Joseph had missed earlier. "Yeah, ya did. I'd ask what you were thinking, but I'm too frustrated to hear your answer right now. And Joseph's right. We have bigger priorities. We need to solve the crisis, and then deal with… whatever is going on with you."

I closed my eyes. I felt empty. Void. My head had gone light, and I was having difficulty focusing. Yet I heard the truth in her words, so I accepted Geoffrey's hand up. My legs were still watery, and he helped steady me for a moment. He then knelt, picked up the trident, and thrust it at me. Only when I took it did he back away.

"I don't care about what you did or why you did it, but you have work to do."

I met his green and gray eyes. Firmed my jaw. "I know."

"I know you do. Now let's go out there and deal with it."

"Ok." I allowed him to get a few yards ahead of me before following suit. Pyra lagged behind, as if to make sure I didn't try to trap myself in this cave. She extinguished the flames she'd lit in the torches as we passed by them. For once, she didn't fill the tense silence with errant chatter.

I wondered if I'd broken more than my relationship with Joseph.

At the entrance of the cave, Geoffrey stopped. He made a strange sound, midway between a gasp and choke, almost seemed to turn back, then toppled over, hands flying to his throat.

It all happened so fast, I wasn't sure I'd seen it correctly.

Pyra shouted, sprinting past me. She glanced at him, shook her head hard, and raced outside. I stopped and knelt, barely registering the pool of red around his body. Beyond him, wiping streaks of red from his scimitar on his pristine robes, stood Oron.

Geoffrey choked again. This time I understood what he said. "Run."

Chapter 23

The earth grumbled. I blasted from the cave with a burst of magic I hadn't felt in some time. As I tumbled to the ground behind Pyra, the door snapped shut, sealing Geoffrey within the tomb.

I felt a pang recalling Geoffrey's words: *only I can get us in.*

With him dead, or almost dead anyway, we would have been trapped. Especially since it appeared Oron had downplayed his abilities.

"What is wrong with you?" Pyra circled the Earth God, both hands on the hilt of her newly acquired sword. Betrayal contorted her face. "Why attack Joseph? And kill Geoffrey? Why?"

Oron didn't answer. Instead, he raised his scimitar, careful to keep both Pyra and me in view. On the other side of him, where Pyra was making her pass, I glimpsed Joseph's prone figure on the ground, arms and legs splayed, both the chakram and my dagger on the ground beyond his reaching fingers.

Heat seared through me, burning away my pain and numbness. Silently, I prayed Joseph wasn't dead, that Oron had only knocked him out.

The scent of smoke caught my attention. Through the gap we'd used to get here, someone screamed, another person shouted an order. Weapons clanged. Someone had set a fire. Lach. Finn. Ryder. I couldn't see them, couldn't distinguish their voices, yet knew something awful had happened.

Oron snapped to face me, his hand coming up—and I reacted.

Pyra shouted as I threw her through the opening through which we'd come mere seconds before it snapped shut with the force of the Earth God's power, sealing Oron, Joseph, and me on one side—and everyone else on the other. Pyra yelled my name and metal sang as she crashed her sword into the stone over and over.

I didn't answer.

"That was clever," Oron signed. "Pushing her along the ground rather than launching her through the air. I didn't expect that."

The trident felt awkward in my grip, despite how easily it fit. I wouldn't be able to use it. I wasn't familiar enough with how it worked. Besides, it wasn't complete without the dagger, so I leaned it against the wall. It wasn't like the Earth God could use it, anyway.

"Why are you doing this, Oron?" I crossed one foot behind the other, slinking around him slowly, hoping to put my body between his and Joseph's. I didn't know if he was alive, but I had to believe he was. Overhead, a fresh wave of purple-bellied clouds rolled over the maze. My magic tingled. We were about to get soaked. "Why this? Why now?"

"Geoffrey was a loose end that should have been eliminated a long time ago." The muscles in Oron's arms bunched as he lowered his center of gravity, watching me, waiting for... I didn't know what. Hopefully, Geoffrey hadn't been lying about this area being secure.

Then again, maybe Oron could control the labyrinth, too.

His fingers flashed again. "And Joseph would have stood in our way at some point. He needed to go. It's too bad, really. I always liked him."

The ground rumbled. I ignited a blast of fire in my palms.

"And I'm deeply sorry for you, too." Oron dropped his scimitar, recognizing this for the battle it was: magic and will over metal and might. "I never wanted it to end like this. I never agreed with Davos's plan, but I am obligated to fulfill my duty."

Seth.

The name rang clear in my mind.

I blinked past the ringing, trying to keep my focus on the threat in front of me despite the thoughts spiraling through my mind. The Earth Temple. They'd been plotting this, planning whatever this was… for Gods knows how long. I didn't have a great idea of what they were thinking, but with Joseph out of the way, it certainly appeared they would, at the very least, take control of the Order. Every uneasy feeling, every uncomfortable gesture, every concern I'd ever had…

Realized.

And Earth's Great Beast—a massive cobra bigger than the White House—it had tried to warn me. Blood whooshed in my ears.

Beware the Desert.

Maybe the Ramalia hadn't meant Phenex. It had never felt right, even after I'd sealed him away and set the nero free. Something had never aligned there—especially when the Beast showed no interest in the djinn.

That's because It had never worried about Phenex.

It had meant the Lost City—home of the Earth Temple.

Davos.

Seth.

And Oron.

A pawn and a puppet in their twisted game.

"What are their orders for me?" I asked. Water surged beneath my feet, coursing through long-forgotten channels woven deep into the mountain. We might be in the center of a stone circle, but we'd walked through plenty of green to get here. Let him think me more concerned about his betrayal. Let him focus on the flames fisted in my hands.

I had more than one trick up my sleeve.

Oron hesitated, his motions jerky, uncertain. Whatever he'd been told to do, I didn't think he wanted to do it. Not deep down. "We're so close to establishing a new Order, a new world, one run the way it should be, with people who know how things should be run in charge."

"I get it. You need the rest of us dead to pull it off." That ripped deep. Not Seth. I'd expected him to pull something at some point. But Oron, a guy who for all his mysteries had appeared to agree with our mission. He'd been a friend to Pyra. And he had—when push came to shove—voiced his true thoughts when they mattered. But this... this told me Davos had sunk its claws into him deep.

Far deeper than I would have ever known.

"I did say I was sorry." Oron seemed to center himself, and a chill skittered up my spine, one of foreboding. "But I've already messed up once, and I can't afford a second failure."

A boulder ripped from the side of the mountain zipped right at me. I shot off a quick blast of wind, knocking it off course enough that it missed my head, brushing my cheek, before it smashed into the ground. I rolled my shoulders, body humming powerfully with magic.

Oron stomped his foot. The ground trembled and the walls quaked. This time, when a group of boulders launched at me from all sides, I was better prepared. A ball of air swirled up around me, a hardened shield of movement that sent the rocks spinning away from me.

The Earth God was already in motion, reaching for more stones to toss at me, but I launched my attack before he could do so. Fire erupted from my hands, the flames ten feet long, and I jumped, more fire pouring from the soles of my feet. Oron's cape swirled and a hardened shell of earth surrounded him, encased him like Air had done for me, easily deflecting my blasts.

No matter. I clapped my hands, summoning the yellow magic to the forefront, spinning up a pair of tornadoes that rapidly grew larger and faster. Oron dropped to his knees, sank his arms into the dirt up to the elbows, and I felt myself... sinking.

Quicksand? Concentration shattered, the howling wind disintegrated as I rushed to freeze the liquid rock sucking at my feet, pulling me down, down, down. I cracked the ice with a hammer of air and stepped out, only to stare up into the rock-face of a giant with dark caverns for eyes and a cracked smile.

Golems.

He'd raised freaking golems.

I ducked the massive fist that swung for my face, hearing the stone whistle as it ripped past my head. A blow that surely would have crushed my skull. I rolled, a bundle of flames whirling around me as I sprang upright, shooting off darts of flame toward the boy in white—only for a second giant to step on the path, absorbing the heat without protest.

Unfortunately, I'd misjudged the second punch the golem threw, and its limestone fist crashed into my side. I slammed into the wall, ribs screaming, barely able to protect the back of my head as dust and debris rained down. There wasn't time to wait and recover, because, for all its weight and heft, the rock soldier moved quickly. Its leg shot out before I had a chance to roll away. The limb crashed into my stomach and I screamed, shards of pain telling me bone had splintered.

No one was more surprised than me when the giant paused, shook, then crumbled, the vibrations of my shriek riddled with magic of sirens, fracturing the rock a hundred different ways. Oron wiped away streaks of blood that wet the cheeks of his mask from his burst eardrums, staring at the mass of rubble that used to be his twin soldiers.

Magic twined around my insides, rushing to heal what was broken, and I lashed out with whips of water, crashing and smashing them against the Earth God. He only allowed one to make contact before calling up another irritating ball of earth that neither water nor ice could pierce.

"Come on out, Oron." I drew a wall of flame around me, abandoning

200

the lackluster liquid. "Why play defense when you're so much better at offense?"

A rockslide crashed into me, sending me tumbling. A fist of earth gripped my arm, pinning me down. I grinned. I had his number now. I opened my mouth, unleashing another siren shriek, shattering the stone. If sound vibrations could do this…

I sensed the sharp spikes of earth rocketing through the air and rolled out of the way, heart slamming against my ribs at another near miss. From above, another boulder dropped, and I barely flung a panel of air up in time to catch it inches from my nose. Its weight felt tremendous as Oron and I fought for greater telekinetic control. My arms shook. Oron would win this fight if I didn't act fast.

"Lights out," I yelled, magic exploding from my body. The world went black, and I used the wind to rocket my way out from beneath the boulder before it crashed. I ran, using my improved hearing to guide my way, knowing I couldn't maintain this level of darkness for very long.

I missed the lip of earth jutting from the ground and tripped, face-planting into another web of quicksand. Daylight flickered back into existence as I flailed in the mud. Like last time, I tried to freeze it, crack it open, but Oron had learned. He maintained the viscosity regardless of the temperature, and I panicked as I sank deeper into the silt.

An inferno boiled within me, and I released it.

The intensity of the heat hardened the earth, and I cracked it with another gasping shriek.

Oron's chest heaved, one hand planted on the side of his head, cradling his ear with one bloodied glove, while the other hovered before him, a silent command to stop. I whipped back my assault of Air before it released, watching him closely. Had he had enough?

No. The God shook his head, his hands clapping together sharply. My stomach dipped. It was a trick. One that nearly worked.

Another boulder flew at my head as the ground trembled beneath my feet, but I flung the mass away. Then another and another, steadily moving backward as my mind cranked out ideas, searching for something that would bring Oron down. My heel kicked against something, sending it clattering behind me. I risked a glance over my shoulder. My dagger. Our attacks must have knocked it over here.

I dropped, snatching up the weapon as another boulder scraped the top of my back. This battle may have started as a war of magics, but I wasn't afraid to end it with steel.

Teeth clenched, I popped upright again, dagger pulled back, prepared to throw, when my foot sank into yet another pool of quicksand, throwing off my balance. I swayed, one foot planted and the other gripped tight. A sense of wrongness engulfed me.

Oron stood there, arms limp at his sides. No more boulders came flying. The lack of... anything from him triggered the chiming of a million bells in my head.

I glanced around as the earth rumbled beneath my feet. Walls. Two walls penned me in on both sides. Only one way forward and one way back. The rumbling grew louder, a sound that I recognized for what it was, a sound I'd spent hours running from.

He'd pushed me into the maze.

Shock sluiced through me, cooling the inferno. Behind Oron, the wall he'd erected between us and the other fey cracked. Ryder appeared in the opening, a mass of swirling dark magic and smoke, his face twisted in a gargoyle snarl.

I tried to run, tried to move, but the quicksand still clung to me, pinning me down. The rumbling grew louder. Heart on my throat, panic blaring through my body, I fought to free my foot, staring in horror first at the wall of Earth Oron put up, blocking my way out...

Then at the crushing mass of rock closing in behind me.

There was no way out.

The Earth enveloped me so quickly, so thoroughly, I didn't feel the agony of being crushed.

Chapter 24

I hadn't known what to expect from death.

Perhaps more pain, maybe less of it. I hadn't lived a particularly sin-free life.

Whatever I'd thought I'd see, total darkness certainly wasn't it.

At least—not total darkness where I retained presence of mind.

Yellow lights popped. Red swirled—followed quickly by ribbons of blue.

Intermixed with them all: green.

You are worthy of Earth.

Ah—there was the pain.

Chapter 25

F*inally.*

Was that me? Kaleal? I couldn't focus on any single thought or sensation. My body quaked with exhaustion, adrenaline, *excitement*—now that the pain was fading. Had faded?

I shuddered, teeth clattering, chilled through and through. I reached out with the hand not clenched around the grip of my weapon, patted the rough surface of the rock. It had contoured to the shape of my body. That explained the dark.

The dark. The labyrinth. I had... it had... I remembered the stone folding around me, pressing in against me, the flare of all-consuming agony...

My legs moved, unbidden.

First things first... let's deal with this pesky nuclear problem.

Kaleal?

My muscles stretched, joints bent. The rock shifted, accommodating this new form. Standing. I couldn't recall wanting to stand. Staying put had seemed like a much better option. Energy pooled in my stomach, spread down my arms, expanding.

My vision fractured. No. Not my vision.

The shell of rock exploded, and I moved through the fragments, batting them aside easily. I felt good, very good. Better than I'd felt in my entire life.

They stared—faces. Familiar faces. I knew those faces.

"Zara?"

I tasted the name on salty, chapped lips. It felt right, yet somehow very wrong. *I* felt wrong. My soul pulsed, my heart thudding in time, aware something didn't seem correct, yet not sure what name to put to it—this sensation.

Magic pulsed. A cool rod slipped through my fingers and I squeezed tight, angling it down. The dagger in my fist fit perfectly in the middle slot, left empty by careful hands. Electricity shot down my spine when it clicked into place. I hefted it over my head, loving how it adapted its weight, its balance, to this body.

My body? Right?

Snapping, violet lightning flickered down the blue-tinted spear, arced over the three toothy points at the crest. A trident. *My* trident.

A trident Ash had designed just for...

Dimly, I heard that word again. That name. Zara. Was that me?

A man with hair of ebony, wrapped in smoke and fear, stepped forward, arm extended. Smudges of red tinted the skin around his tiger stone eyes, which flickered between relief and desperation. My head canted, silvery hair spilling over my shoulder. Hummingbirds fluttered in my chest, beating helplessly against my ribs. I knew him, knew this—

You'll have time to deal with him after. But first, we have work to do.

We. We was good. We didn't feel so... alone.

With the faces of those around me forgotten, my heel slammed into the ground. A chunk broke away. I stood tall as we drifted up and up and up, staff firm in my grasp, thoughts flicking back and forth on a pendulum's arc. *What work?*

Magic crackled. A pesky shield tried to hold me back. I imagined it was supposed to hurt, pressing against my palm like this, energy snapping angrily, viciously. How irritating, this magic, keeping me from what I needed to do.

Which was what again?

Soon.

The bowl of energy shattered into a million shards of multi-colored light. Uninhibited once more, my elevator of rock drifted farther up, following the sharp incline of the mountain. Higher and higher, the wispy, ugly clouds dispersing as I joined them, scattering like silverfish in a pond.

Body light and soul nimble, I stepped from my platform to the mountain. The earth crumbled, flaking and cracking as it tumbled down to the world below.

The world... below.

In the distance bloomed four domed clouds, slender in the bottom and wide at the top. They didn't disperse like the cirrus clouds I handled so effortlessly. As I stared at the white puffy tops and the flashing red and yellow heat dancing across their cores...

I recalled a vision. Not mine. But words murmured by someone else.

I saw you ushering in the world's final moments.

Words that weren't mine, yet seemed to fit...

Geoffrey.

The dream state in which I floated cracked, and I crashed into my body. It was too much. Too much to process, too much sensation. Lightning crackled over my knuckles, the trident begging for me to use it, but I could barely think as the nuclear blasts doubled, tripled before me.

The world as I knew it was ending.

And I stood here, trident in hand, watching.

Do something. We're the only one who can, Kaleal urged.

"I don't know what to do." The words tumbled past my numb lips. It was over. All over. "It's too late."

It's never too late, the God snarled. *There is still time, if you let me show you how.*

No. I didn't want to, but I also didn't want it all to end. Not like this. "Tell me what to do," I ordered in a rush. "Tell me and I'll do it."

In the distance, the nuclear mushrooms blossomed higher, wider.

It's too much for me to tell, Kaleal snapped. *Too much you could get wrong. I need to help you or this won't work.*

"I'm not letting you out."

Then I'm not helping. Let your world crumble. The God sank back, arms folded. *I'll survive this, but you won't. Your friends won't.*

I hated that I didn't know if that was true, that she might somehow survive. She had an uncanny ability for it, after all.

And in this game of chicken, she was definitely winning.

I didn't want to agree, didn't want to give her so much as an inch. But I didn't know how to use this weapon. I didn't understand what it did. How it worked. How revival could play any sort of role in solving this problem.

I would have to give her some leeway, but not too much.

I steeled myself. I would have to maintain enough energy to push her back behind my barricades again. It was a risk, but the only risk I could afford to take.

"Fine," I gritted. "Show me what to do." I lowered my barriers partway, everything inside me screaming that this was wrong. That I shouldn't be doing this.

But it was already done.

Kaleal guided me forward, angled the trident over my head, and together we brought it crashing down. Words I didn't know, had never heard before, spilled from my lips. *"Kala lee, mekka quo. E mezetro. E mezero. Ne."*

Magic I'd grown used to handling, had always treated as a familiar friend, now ripped from me, cut me open, visible scars cracked and bleeding as it abused my battered body and funneled into the weapon.

My vision went white.

And still I held on, teeth jammed together, fists clenched as I held the staff steady, prongs rooted in the ground, funneling everything of me into everything that remained of the world. It hit me then, what Kaleal was doing. The magical core of the world, the one that went dormant when the Gods vanished from the surface, the one that slowly pulsed back to life when they revived, the one that inhibited technological advancement as magic took over...

She was reviving it to full strength, fast-forwarding a process that should have taken at least a decade to complete.

She was giving the world the power it needed to save itself.

Before my eyes, the mushroom clouds dissipated, like they'd been drawn into a filter. I knew it for what it was... the earth healing.

But at what cost... and what consequence? Both for the planet and for myself?

Magic bled from me, bright as starlight and smooth as whispers, breathing life into the earth.

And she responded, reclaiming control over her own destiny, her own fate. With a thought, she pushed the fingers of technology and human advancement from her flesh and embraced the proper nature of our world that was... magic.

I knew we'd gone too far, farther than I'd ever thought possible, yet I couldn't stop. Sobs ripped from my lungs as the last of my energy ebbed, seeping into the earth like so much spilled ink. When she bled me dry, then, and only then, did she release me.

The staff tumbled from my limp fingers, clattered against the stones, and shattered. The effort of what I'd done had leeched the fragments of their vibrant color, staining the metal white. I slumped against a curved rock, arm hooked over the top to keep myself upright. I had nothing more, nothing left to give. My energy, my magic, my soul...

All gone.

And it was then, in my weakest moment…
I felt an icy chill wash through my core.
I felt *her* moving in.

Chapter 26

Whom it came to prying my soul from my shell, Kaleal worked meticulously.

She would tear a small portion of my soul away from my body, then clear the surface left behind, erasing the memory of *me* from my muscles and bones. As she worked, she replaced the areas my soul used to fill with her own.

My head lolled, bringing the deep green forest of Aldiirin into view. When Kaleal finished her work, my soul wouldn't even be a memory inside myself.

It's nothing personal, Kaleal said, tone matter-of-fact. *You happened to be the vessel through with I redeem my legacy.*

I reached for my magic. Came up short.

"You say that, but it feels deeply personal," I replied through numb lips, too tired to engage in a verbal battle. My leg twitched, absent of me moving it.

She paused, coffin nails suspended over a piece of my soul. *I suppose it is a little personal. You tried to shut me away—several times.*

A bird, dark as the tendrils of whatever nothingness had eaten away at Ridley's mind, soared overhead. Its body cast a shadow beside me. I rolled my head to follow it. At my side lay the broken bits of the trident. The strain of what we'd done—the miracle we'd pulled off—must have been too much for it. Amid the shards lay my dagger. The base of it was dinged and a little cracked, but mostly it was intact.

"So the prophecy is real." I curled my fingers, surprised I retained that much control.

Hardly.

I couldn't feel one of my legs. Kaleal had successfully severed my soul's grip on that part of myself. I couldn't remember what it felt like to possess that part of my body. She was smart, doing what she was doing. This way, if I were to get free from her hold, I wasn't sure my soul would be able to re-attach to its physical form.

I hoped. I dreamed. But you, the miracle that is you, it's pure coincidence. And I've never turned away an opportunity to use coincidence to my advantage.

The bird swung by again, its left wing crooked.

"If you knew what I would become, why not take control and accomplish what you needed yourself?" I wanted to fight. I wanted to beat her back. But I felt so tired. And holding her back now, when she seemed so invincible, felt like a lot of work. "It would have taken less time."

Kaleal chuckled. *I waited thousands of years. What were a few more months? Besides, you proved truly resilient; I would admire you if I didn't resent you.*

I felt admiration and resentment fit hand-in-hand but didn't press the issue.

And if you recall, I did try to take control, several times.

I wondered if she'd tried to steal control as far back as Kansas City.

But you always pulled some magic out of your metaphorical cap. Clearly, the fates intended for you to do this all on your own... with a few nudges along the way. She whistled through her teeth. *I don't interfere with the fates.*

So she did fear someone.

A thought occurred to me. "What was the cost of using the weapon?

It's cursed, right?"

Kaleal chuckled. *Memories. And you won't know which ones. It's such a wonderful balance, don't you think? Imagine reviving a loved one... only to find the curse erased your memory of them entirely. It's so deeply poetic.*

I swallowed, sorrow clicking in my throat, wondering what I wouldn't remember, wondering if it had cost Kaleal her memories, too.

Granted, given the amount of energy we'd poured into the world, I was surprised, in that case, I remembered anything at all.

Something large thudded heavily on the rock nearby. I pitied whoever or whatever it was, because unless they slit my throat now, they would have a very real and very vengeful Kaleal on their hands. My cheek twitched as I tried to look, couldn't summon the energy.

Couldn't find it in me to be frustrated about it.

"It's her." Finn. I still knew him, at least. He'd found me. But why? What was the point? The world was saved from one disaster. I only wished I could have prevented the nightmare that may prove far worse.

"Glowstick."

I closed my eyes, awash in the relief I hadn't forgotten Ryder, either.

Gravel clattered as the incubus dropped to my side, his hands folding me into him. My heart fluttered, a tiny spark of life flickering faintly. I would miss him. The incubus squeezed my limp hand, fingers finding my pulse.

"Get out of here." Talking to Kaleal had been so easy. Yet now the words settled like a mantle in the back of my throat. "You need to get far away from here."

Miraculously, Kaleal didn't seem to mind them being here. She was far too focused on taking control. Or, perhaps, a small scrap of humanity lingered inside her twisted being, one that would allow me to say these final goodbyes.

Ryder ignored my plea and pulled me into his lap, as if trying to touch as much of me to as much of him as he could. "Why would you say that? You stopped the apocalypse. It's time to get you home to—"

"I won't be going home." I could barely feel my lungs. "It's over for me. Maybe for all of you, too."

"I don't understand." Ryder cradled my neck as his arm supported my back. His golden eyes swept across my form feverishly. Oh, Ryder. If only we'd had more time. "What's wrong?"

Finn stroked my arm, bending low over Ryder's shoulder. "Come on, we got this—"

"I can't hold her off, not any longer." I breathed in the intoxicating mix of scents that was *him,* knowing this was the last time I would enjoy Ryder as myself. Ever. "Kaleal is too strong, too determined, and I'm tapped out. I have nothing left."

"No." Ryder's arms tensed, the veins in his neck corded. "You've held her off before. You can do it now."

"I'm so tired." I broke his gaze to smile wanly at Finn, his normally tan face pale as moonstone. "I have nothing left to fight her with. I saved the world from itself, now it will need to save itself... from her."

"No—"

I winced, lifted one arm, the arm I could still feel, and pressed a finger to Ryder's lips, trailed my nails across his stubbled cheek. "You need to get as far away from here as you can. Warn the world what's coming, because they need to be prepared."

I hated saying these words, hated how Kaleal's ego swelled with satisfaction, but I didn't dare give anyone an opportunity to underestimate her. Not again. Never again.

I fumbled with the chain around my neck, found the vial, snapped it off. The silver warmed beneath my touch, but I didn't dare linger, instead offering it to Finn, who accepted it with the broken expression of a man who was watching his life slip away before his eyes.

"Take Phenex." Kaleal snapped my control over my arm and it

dropped, deadened. "And go. She has all four elements. You know what kind of damage she'll be able to do."

"I'm not leaving you." Ryder lifted my face to his, swept his thumb across my hairline. "You can't ask that of me."

"I can and I will." Darkness tinged the far corners of my vision. "You need to go while you can. I can't help you anymore." It killed me to say that, to realize this was happening, that Kaleal was going to win.

At my side, I watched my fingers twitch. I knew what that meant, what would come next.

Kaleal was trying out her newfound home. Once she severed my mind, I knew she wouldn't hesitate to attack them. My eyes shot to Finn's. "Go. Now. She's almost free."

Unlike Ryder, Finn understood what I was saying. He would make sure they survived. He had to.

My ears buzzed. I couldn't hear him as he grabbed Ryder, as he ripped the incubus upright, their faces mired with anguish. My vision faded. I didn't see them make their escape.

Didn't know if they'd gotten away—at all.

Like it? Love it? Want more of it? Leave a review! I want to know what you think.
A few words can change the world.

Book Five Coming Soon

You didn't think I'd leave you hanging forever, did you?? The thrilling conclusion to Zara's, Ryder's, Finn's, Kaleal's, Lachlan's, Pyra's, Oron's, Joseph's—everyone's!—story is in the works right now.

In the meantime… stay up-to-date with the latest release information by signing up for my monthly newsletter! In those, you'll discover book updates and free, exclusive content related to both The Elemental Gods series and my other work. To find out more, head to www.septembert homas.com.

Books by September Thomas

The Elemental Gods
Walk on Water
Fan the Flame
Wind and Reign
War of Earth

Acknowledgements

Just over two years ago I launched headfirst into this whole author thing and haven't looked back. The joy of writing and the pleasure that comes with crafting characters and worlds—is insurmountable. This series has swept me up and carried me away...

And it wouldn't have been possible without the support of everyone around me.

Fiona—your scheming mind never fails to turn this story (and its poor, beleaguered characters) on its head. I adore your ability to take (highly significant) issues I've wrangled with for days on end... and put them to rights in minutes. Without your (not so) gentle nudges, I'd probably still be trapped dodging landmines in chapters nine and twelve.

Natasha—you've outdone yourself yet again. High-fives on another brilliant cover. I dare say Sha would preen if she could see her portrait.

Josh—you've earned many boxes of baseball cards listening to me twist and turn and hem and haw over every single detail... only to turn around and rethink everything again the next day. No matter how many weekends we stay home or how many evenings we cut short so I can haunt a computer screen in the early morning, you never complain. If I didn't love you for so many other reasons already, that alone would take a starring role.

David—I'm dying to hear what you think of WOE. I know your investment in these characters. Please don't hate me too much for that ending.

Mom and Dad—thank you for sharing the mountains and valleys that come with writing. I love you both so much.

To you, my readers - and all my friends - keep being the amazingly awesome people all of you are.

And, of course, Sydney. You've sat with me through every nuance, each individual word, never understanding exactly why I choose to do what I do, but accepting of it all the same. You're the sweetest chunk, the most cuddly fluff—yes, I'll give you some popcorn since you're staring at me.

About the Author

September Thomas is the author of the Elemental Gods series. She lives in Nebraska with her boyfriend and rescued Australian Cattle Dog. She also boasts a large collection of (fake) owls that some consider amusingly ridiculous.

You can connect with me on:

🌐 https://www.septemberthomas.com

📘 https://www.facebook.com/SeptemberThomasAuthor

🔗 https://www.instagram.com/september.thomas

🔗 https://www.pinterest.com/september_thomas

Subscribe to my newsletter:

✉ https://www.septemberthomas.com

www.ingramcontent.com/pod-product-compliance
Lightning Source LLC
Chambersburg PA
CBHW060919180626
46817CB00004B/1321